Kate —

Big Easy Heat

Happy Reading!

Mari Carr

Mari Carr

Copyright © 2014 Mari Carr

All rights reserved.

ISBN: 150109047X
ISBN-13: 978-1501090479

CONTENTS

Acknowledgments   i

Blank Canvas   1

Crash Point   125

ACKNOWLEDGMENTS

I would like to thank RG Alexander, Eden Bradley and Lauren Hawkeye for including me in their group projects (Midnight Ink and Riding Desire). Without these invitations, the Big Easy series would not have been born.

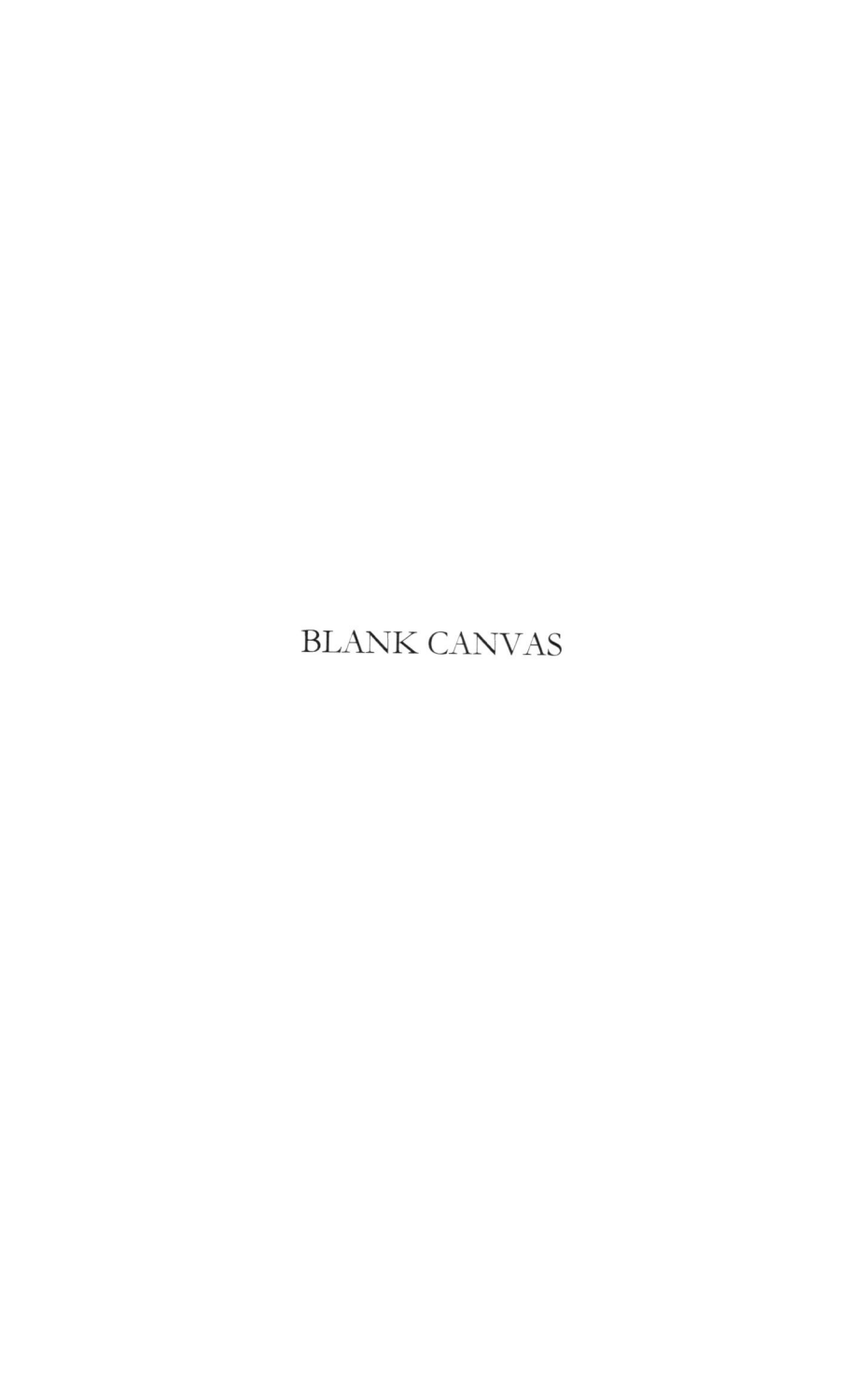

BLANK CANVAS

CHAPTER ONE

Jennifer O'Neal released a long sigh as she stared at the front door of Midnight Ink. What the hell was she doing here? She wasn't this kind of person. Was she? The kind who called in sick to work to get a tattoo? The type who wore a tube-top in public? The sort who allowed some stranger to cover her back in ink?

No. She wasn't.

And that was the problem.

Marcus' voice drifted back to her.

I'm bored. Day after day of the same thing, Jennifer. I wake up every morning thinking there's gotta be more to life than this.

At the time, the words—when paired with *I've met someone else*—had cut through her like a machete. She'd been maimed, mortally wounded, devastated.

There was security in familiarity and after seventeen

years of marriage, she and Marcus were about as familiar as it got. Their lives had fallen into a very comfortable routine. Maybe they didn't talk as much as they had in the early days of their relationship, maybe they didn't set the sheets on fire, but that didn't mean she didn't love him. For her, trading passion and excitement for a safe, reliable future with the man who had become her best friend had been worth it.

Marcus hadn't felt the same.

Which left her here. In front of a tattoo shop in the middle of Canal Street on a Tuesday morning taking advantage of a "New Beginnings" sale.

This was a mistake. She started to turn around, but before she could take the first step, the front door opened and a bell jangled, drawing her from her thoughts.

"Jennifer?"

She nodded mutely as she stared at Caliph, the artist she'd met with briefly the day after New Year's when they'd sat down to design her tattoo.

He was another reason she'd found it so difficult to return. He was the exact description of every man her mother had ever warned her to stay the hell away from. Tall and rough-looking, with a shaved head and muscular arms covered in bright tattoos, he was intimidating and overwhelming with an air of danger that made her stomach feel funny things that had nothing to do with fear and everything to do with sex. Which was weird because she hadn't felt those kinds of stirrings in a few years. Jesus.

Maybe it was closer to a decade.

Caliph grinned when it became obvious she wasn't going to speak. "I thought that was you. Reconsidering?"

She started to shake her head no, then stopped and shrugged. "I don't know."

He stepped to the side and gestured toward the shop. "Wanna come in and talk about it? No pressure. You won't be the first person to change their mind and I promise it won't hurt my feelings if you do. Tattoos are forever, so it's smart to be completely positive."

"Okay."

She managed to take the steps required, pausing only briefly once she was next to him. The man had her by at least a foot and a hundred pounds. He was massive.

"Good girl," he murmured with a genuine smile as he placed his hand on her lower back and gently directed her inside the older building. She tried to repress the shiver his soft touch provoked. "Let's grab a cup of coffee, then we'll snag some seats in the reception area. I haven't hit my quota of caffeine for the day, so your cold feet are coming in handy. Giving me a chance to polish off another cup or three."

Another artist looked over at them as they walked past and pointed to Caliph with narrowed eyes. "You finish that pot again without making another one and I'll kick your ass."

"That might actually be a threat if you had a hope in

hell of beating me in a fight, Shep. But, of course, you don't," Caliph teased.

Jennifer eyed the other artist, taking in his equally impressive height and the wicked scar on his brow. She wasn't sure she shared Caliph's confidence. Then she studied Caliph's Mr. Universe-sized physique and suspected if nothing else, it would be one hell of a fight.

The receptionist—Sassy—looked up from her seat behind the front desk as Caliph and Shep were talking. The last time Jennifer had visited Midnight Ink, the streak in Sassy's hair had been hot pink. Today, it was a vivid red that brought out that same color in the tattooed roses on her full sleeves. "Wow. If that isn't the pot calling the kettle black. Shep, you're one to talk about leaving the pot empty. I'm starting to think I'm the only one in the place who knows how to work the machine."

Shep grinned at her. "But your coffee is the best, Sassy."

Sassy shot him a dirty look. "Don't even try that line on me. You're the king of bullshit and I know it. I'm heading out to run a couple of errands, so you two are on your own for a while. Rosie is coming in later this afternoon. Y'all need anything?"

Caliph and Shep both said no.

"You good, Jennifer?"

Jennifer nodded, surprised the receptionist remembered her name. She'd only been in the shop once before and even that visit had been brief. "I'm fine. Thanks."

Sassy stopped at the front door and gave her an encouraging grin. "You're in good hands, baby doll. Caliph is one of the best." With that, she left.

"You want some coffee?" Caliph offered when they reached the pot. "Sassy really does make the best brew in the state of Louisiana."

She shook her head. She was already too keyed up, on edge. Coffee would only make that condition worse.

Caliph poured himself a cup and winked as he put the now-empty pot back. Then he led her back to the reception area, waiting until she sat down. He grabbed the seat next to her, chuckling. "You'd think after six years of being my best friend, Shep would know better than to tell me what to do. I'm just ornery enough to always do the opposite."

She laughed lightly at his joke. Then Jennifer was struck by how wrong the stereotypes about tattooed guys in leather were in regards to Caliph. How many women would walk by him on the street and feel genuine fear? Hell, she probably would have felt the same way prior to meeting him. She would have reached into her purse to wrap her hand around the can of pepper spray, not relaxing her white-knuckled grip on it until Caliph was well out of sight.

That realization made her feel guilty.

Caliph stretched out his legs, filling their tiny corner.

She grinned.

"What?" he asked.

"You're huge. It's like you take up every spare inch of space and then some."

He laughed, clearly not offended by her observation. "Yeah. Hit my growth spurt at fourteen. Spent the next four years turning down the high school football coach who begged me to play. Jesus, the guy tried everything from bribery to threats. I think he even cried once. He couldn't understand why a kid my size would spend his afternoons in the art room, drawing stupid pictures, rather than on the gridiron."

"Looks like you had the last laugh. You've made a career of art."

Caliph leaned forward. "You don't know the half of it. Fate is a bitch with a wicked sense of humor and I think she likes me. Few years ago, that coach showed up here and I gave him his first tat. He's been back three times since for more ink."

"Bet he's glad you spent the time honing your skills now."

"Yeah, but the truth is nobody was surprised when I started doing tattoos. Been drawing pictures since the cradle, according to my mom."

Jennifer had looked through a portfolio of his work.

It was beautiful, a lot of his artwork simple and colorful. It was the main reason she'd selected him to do her tattoo. Midnight Ink was known as one of the best shops in New Orleans, with a reputation for cleanliness and incredible designs.

"Must be nice to have a job where you can put your talents to work."

He nodded. "It is. What do you do, Jennifer?"

"I'm the manager of Le Chateau Bayonne."

Caliph's eyebrows rose. "Hey, that's a classy hotel. Man, I'd love to see the inside of that place. Heard about the European décor. I know a guy who stayed there once. Super pricy apparently, but he said it was the best bed he's ever slept in."

Jennifer was flattered by his comment, even as she considered the hotel's typical clientele. Caliph hadn't exaggerated. The nightly room rates were more than she paid in one month's rent for her crappy apartment.

After the divorce, she and Marcus had sold their three-bedroom home, neither of them able to afford the mortgage on their own, let alone buy the other person out. So, she'd been uprooted from her nice, friendly neighborhood and thrust back into the world of paying rent on a lousy, too-tiny apartment in a less than desirable part of town.

In some ways, it rubbed against the grain to spend her days surrounded by people for whom money wasn't a concern while she was constantly counting her pennies, sticking to a budget. Her salary was okay—pretty good by most standards—but it was tough adjusting to living on one paycheck after years of sharing the load with Marcus and his teaching pay.

"It really is beautiful inside—French doors, gabled windows, wrought iron balconies. If you ever want a tour of the hotel, just let me know."

Caliph's face lit up. "Seriously? Because yeah, I wouldn't mind seeing it."

Jennifer was happy to have something cool to offer. Caliph was fascinating to her on about a million different levels, which made her feel like the Queen of Dullsville.

Then she realized her stomach was no longer twisted in knots and her fears over getting the tattoo fell away. Caliph had promised not to pressure her and he hadn't. Hell, he hadn't even mentioned the ink. He'd simply sat down and talked to her until her nervousness faded away.

"I'd like to get the tattoo," she said quietly.

"Hell yeah, that's my girl. Come on." He offered a hand to help her rise, then led her to his corner of the shop, the wooden floors creaking along the way. Jennifer studied each station they passed as a means of distraction. Brightly colored Mardi Gras beads adorned one, while Caliph's was much simpler. Sparse actually. Just an old family photo sat in a frame next to his equipment.

"Did you eat breakfast like I said?" Caliph asked.

She nodded. The toast she'd consumed had tasted like sawdust, but she'd choked it down.

"Pretty blouse. Take it off."

She'd covered the tube top she'd bought especially for today with a blouse. She'd had to force herself to keep the top four buttons open because she didn't want to look like a complete prude in front of Caliph.

She could have walked down the street in just the tube top as it was unseasonably warm. You had to love January in New Orleans. The temperature could be fifty degrees one day and eighty the next. For the past few days, they'd been riding in the upper seventies with blue skies and full sunshine that made it feel even hotter.

Despite the gorgeous weather, it had been uncomfortable for her to walk out of her apartment, sans bra, in the revealing outfit. She wasn't exactly lacking in the breast department and the only time she took off her double D bra was in the privacy of her own home.

She tugged the blouse off, folding and placing it on a nearby chair, sighing softly as she acknowledged the blouse was far from pretty and much closer to plain. The best description for her wardrobe was conservative. She did a mental eye roll. That was being nice. The truth was her clothing—like her—was boring.

God, why couldn't she shake that word from her vocabulary? Marcus had walked out on her almost a year earlier. It was time to let it go.

It was actually the arrival of the final divorce papers in the mail shortly before Christmas—*happy holidays to me*, she thought sardonically—that had jarred her out of her numb state and convinced her she needed to do something unpredictable and adventurous. When New Year's Eve arrived, she'd decided—with the help of a bottle of Pinot Grigio—this would be the year she sorted her shit out. She was going to break free of her same old routine and force herself to try different things.

Unfortunately, so far, the wildest thing she'd conjured up was getting this tattoo. She was so lame.

She glanced at the table before her.

"You're going to lie on your stomach, Jen. I need to sit down to work. I'm steadier that way."

She blushed as she crawled onto the table. She wasn't sure why, but the position made her feel vulnerable. Maybe it was because her dirty mind had invented too many fantasies the past two weeks about her getting horizontal with the gentle giant currently looming over her.

Then she considered how he'd shortened her name, calling her Jen. It was something only her family and closest friends did and it made her feel more at ease.

He didn't speak again as he put her into the position he wanted, lowering her tube top a wee bit as he lightly touched and cleaned her skin. She'd elected to have the tattoo put on her upper back, near her right shoulder. That way it would be hidden beneath her clothing. The owner of the hotel didn't have a policy about managers and tattoos, but that was probably because she seemed like the person least likely to ever get one. Even so, she didn't want to test the theory. She needed her job.

Then she recalled her wardrobe once more. With the exception of when she went swimming, this tat would probably *never* see the light of day. Bare skin wasn't part of her repertoire.

Neither of them spoke as he sprayed liquid soap to the spot and transferred the image on her skin. Jennifer took the time to study his face as he concentrated on his work, his warm hands gently smoothing the paper over her skin. It occurred to her she didn't have a clue how old he was. His face was tanned; his jaw covered with dark stubble that indicated he probably hadn't shaved this morning. There were laugh lines around his eyes she had the irresistible urge to run her fingertips over. The man could be anywhere between twenty-five and forty.

His fingers felt like magic, firing up some hot buttons that had lain dormant for far too long. She struggled to pull air into her lungs.

Caliph must have mistaken her arousal for nervousness. "Relax, beauty. You don't want to tense your muscles like that. The reality of this is it's going to hurt, but if you could loosen up a little, it'll be easier for you."

"Okay," she whispered, closing her eyes and cursing her suddenly tight throat, afraid of how she'd react to the pain. She wanted this damn tattoo. She really did. So why was she acting like a scared mouse? Why couldn't she summon even an ounce of bravery? Caliph probably thought she was a wuss.

He leaned closer. "Jen. Look at me."

She opened her eyes, trying not to reveal what his close proximity did to her. Mercifully, her position facedown on the table hid the fact her nipples had just gone hard, but it was more difficult to shield her flushing face and accelerated breathing.

He stroked her cheek gently with one finger. She pressed her legs together, trying to calm her arousal. Her pussy clenched hungrily and her panties were definitely damp.

"I'm finished with the sketch. Now comes the hard part. If it starts to be too much, tell me to stop and I will."

"Should I have a safe word?" She'd meant the words as a risqué joke, amazed she'd found the balls for off-color humor, but something about Caliph made her think *Dom*.

After her husband walked out, Jennifer had turned to books—reading voraciously for hours each night after work. Her love for historical romances soon drifted toward the erotic genre when the sweet, closed-door love scenes stopped doing it for her. She'd gone through a shifter phase, then a ménage one. These days she couldn't get enough of BDSM stories.

Caliph's gaze darkened and Jennifer reconsidered her previous assessment about his gentle personality. This man was no puppy dog. He was pure Pit Bull. Foolishly, that discovery didn't make her want to run. It only ramped up her desires even more.

"I was just kidding," she hastily added. "Very bad joke."

Caliph didn't reply, didn't let her off the hook easily. She fought the desire to stand and walk out of the shop. What on earth had possessed her to make such an inappropriate comment to a virtual stranger? She'd always considered common sense one of her better traits. Where the hell had that gone?

Finally, a slight smile tipped his lips. "You're an interesting woman, Jen. I like that."

Interesting? It was on the tip of her tongue to correct his misapprehension. He'd just caught her on a good day.

"You ready?" he asked.

She nodded once, then braced herself for the first pierce of the needle.

He'd warned her about the pain, but holy shit!

"Ohmigod! Jesus Christ! Fuck me!"

Caliph chuckled. "If you insist."

It took a second for the haze of pain to clear enough for her to understand his joke.

She glared at him. "That hurt."

"Never said it wouldn't. You wanna go on?"

No. She didn't. But as Caliph said, fate was a wicked bitch and she chose that moment to arrive and bless Jennifer with courage. Or was it pride?

"Yes," she replied through gritted teeth.

Once again, he murmured his standard good girl, the compliment inciting an unfamiliar warmth inside her.

The tattoo gun fired up again, provoking another long stream of curse words to fly from her lips. Caliph grinned, but he didn't stop this time.

For several moments, he worked in silence as Jennifer tried to adapt to the pain. The initial hurt had started to wane and soon she learned to regulate her breathing as she anticipated his moves. Before too long, the buzz of the gun turned to white noise and she actually became drowsy.

Caliph must have sensed when she'd finally managed to relax because he broke the silence, his question rousing her just before she drifted off.

"Why a daisy?"

She jerked slightly and he apologized softly.

"Sorry. Were you falling asleep?"

She shook her head, lying so he wouldn't feel bad. "No."

He repeated the question. "Why a daisy tattoo?"

Jennifer considered her response, wishing he hadn't

asked. The real reason was too personal, too revealing, too damn girly. She didn't want to know what Caliph would think if she told him the truth.

"It's my favorite flower." That much was true. Maybe that would be enough of a reason for him.

Unfortunately the man was too astute. "You don't have to tell me if you don't want to."

She frowned, feeling an odd need to protest his dismissal. "It really is my favorite."

"I'm sure it is. How old are you?"

She tried to understand his bizarre switch in subjects. "I'm going to be forty in August."

He smiled. "You know, most women would have said thirty-nine rather than confess to hitting the big four-oh so soon."

She considered the truth of that. "Forty is coming whether I admit it or not."

Her answer pleased him. She could see it in his expression. It increased the warmth inside her, leaving her confused about why his happiness left her feeling so content, gratified.

"Glad to hear you're not one of those women who has issues with age."

Jennifer winced slightly when his needle poked a sore spot. Suddenly she was glad for the distraction of conversation. "Nope. No sense fighting the inevitable. Besides I'm sort of looking forward to getting the hell out of my thirties." She'd spent most of that decade with Marcus and look how well that turned out. She'd started this year determined to make some changes, so why not start with a new number in front of her age?

"Good for you." Caliph picked up something from his tray, but Jennifer averted her eyes. There was a big difference between knowing there was a needle jabbing into her skin and seeing said needle. "Which leads me back to my original question. Why a daisy?"

She tried to dodge answering with an inquiry of her own. "Why did you want to know how old I was?"

His eyes never left the site of the tattoo. She found his intense concentration sexy as hell.

Jesus, lock the hormones away, Jennifer. Pretty soon you'll start drooling.

"It's not unusual for women to get a tattoo when those big birthdays start looming, but for most of them, I think it's a way to pretend the clock isn't ticking. It's their attempt to turn back time. You don't seem to care about age, so clearly that's not the impetus for this tat."

Impetus? Tattoo artist armchair psychiatry. "Where did you go to school?" She didn't specify high school or college on the off chance she was wrong and she'd somehow offend him.

"ULM."

Nope, not wrong. College grad. She tried to school her features, but she didn't fool him.

He chuckled. "Surprised to find out your tattoo artist has a bachelor's degree?"

She shook her head as more of the stereotypes fell away. God. Was she really so narrow-minded?

"It's okay, Jen. Tattoo artists aren't obligated to get a degree in art. That requirement came from my mother. She'd preached about the importance of a college education from the day I was born until I graduated from high school and nothing short of a zombie apocalypse was going to be a good enough excuse not to further my education."

"She sounds scary. And awesome."

He stopped working for a moment to capture her gaze. "You're right. She's both. But enough of that. You keep changing the subject. If you don't want to tell me what the daisy represents, just say 'fuck off.'"

Even with his permission, she'd never say that to him. Probably because part of her was afraid he would and she didn't like the thought of him leaving.

She shook that thought out of her head instantly. She was just getting a tattoo from the guy, not dating him.

"I don't understand why you keep insisting there's some deep meaning behind it. Can't I just like a flower?"

"You've left this soft, pale skin untouched for thirty-nine years. You don't strike me as the impulsive type. I'd be willing to bet you're a planner, a list maker. Someone who thinks before they act. You're also intelligent and sensitive. There's a story behind the daisy."

His astute observations left her speechless. He was right. She'd spent countless hours pouring over images of tattoos as she considered what was right for her. When she'd seen the delicate rendering of the daisy with several of its petals lightly drifting down, it had spoken to her, felt right.

"My husband left me for another woman last year." She hadn't intended to speak the words aloud. In fact, she could count on one hand the number of times she'd actually admitted to Marcus' desertion. A few close friends knew the truth. As for the rest of her acquaintances, she'd used the tried and true *we just drifted apart* lie.

"What a jackass."

Caliph had muttered his reply, but his vehemence caught her off-guard. She giggled.

"Don't move," he instructed, lifting the tattoo gun away.

She apologized as she struggled to compose herself again.

"Thanks. Jackass fits," she said after he'd resumed his work.

"Don't thank me. I'm just stating a fact."

More warmth. More happiness. So much in fact, she wondered if there was some narcotic in the ink that was drugging her senses, serving as an aphrodisiac.

"I've spent the last year trying to figure out what I did wrong."

Caliph turned off the gun, frowning. "*He* had the affair and you think *you* did something wrong?"

"People who are happily married don't stray."

"Maybe not, but fucking someone else is a surefire way *not* to fix the marriage."

His strong opinions made her curious. "Have you ever been married?"

He released a long sigh. "No, Jen, I haven't. Marriage isn't really something I aspire to. But that doesn't mean I don't understand. I've had a couple long-term relationships go south. Maybe there weren't wedding rings on our fingers, but I was committed just the same."

"I'm saying this badly. Marcus and I were together for seventeen years. Long enough for me to start becoming complacent, maybe even a little lazy. In the future, I won't take my relationships for granted."

"I get that, but I don't like that you're blaming yourself."

"My ex was an asshole. The way he chose to leave was cowardly and wrong. I'm not denying that, but it would be very shallow and shortsighted of me to pretend it was all his fault. Takes two to tango."

"That still doesn't explain the tat."

"I've spent the past year feeling like complete dog shit."

Caliph chuckled at her description; his eyes were brimming with compassion.

"I got my divorce papers just before the holidays and they sort of woke me up. Jerked me out of my depression."

"Doesn't sound like a bad thing."

She released a long breath, wondering why she found it so easy to talk to Caliph. "It wasn't. I spent the last year dwelling on the negative, feeling sorry for myself. This year, I'm going for the positive. That's where the daisy comes in."

Caliph's brow creased. "How?"

She smiled when she considered her reason. "It's going to be my reminder that we don't get just one shot at happiness in life. Marcus loved me. Then he loved me not."

Caliph pressed a soft finger to a spot on her back. Though she couldn't see it, she suspected it was one of the petals that had fallen from the flower.

"There are a lot more petals on that flower." Maybe it would sound silly to Caliph, but to her the reason for getting this tattoo made sense. "I have a lot more chances to find my happily ever after."

"You think you need a man to be happy?"

She shook her head. "No. Not at all." She'd heard the same argument from her girlfriends for months. They were full of well-meaning advice, telling her to take time for herself, enjoy life on her own. Hell, she was pretty sure half the married ones were jealous of her single state, wishing for their own freedom.

"I don't have to be in a relationship to feel good about myself. I got knocked down a peg when Marcus left and I've been trying to find my balance since then. I'm still a bit wobbly, but I'm getting there. Being in love has nothing to do with that."

Caliph looked like he might argue, but she cut him off.

"I've spent the last year living on my own. Can I do it? Yeah, sure. I just don't want to. I loved being married and I looked forward to growing old with someone. It's not something I need, Caliph. It's just something I want. A man to talk to about my day, to eat dinner with, to fight over the remote with. His side of the bed, my side. Twice the laundry and dishes. Sharing the bills, splitting dessert in a restaurant. The good and the bad. I miss it."

He smiled at her. "You might be the first person on earth to actually make marriage sound good to me."

She laughed. "So you're really not a fan of marriage at

all?"

He shrugged. "Not sure I've ever considered it one way or the other. I've always been pretty happy with my status quo."

Jennifer felt a twinge of envy. She hadn't enjoyed much about her life for the past year. No, it was more than that. If she was being honest, she'd been just as miserable and bored in her marriage to Marcus as her ex had been with her. Only she'd been too afraid—or was it lazy?—to do anything about it.

"Well, I'm certainly not looking to get married again right away. That's a plan for some distant future. For now, I'm hoping to find a way to shed some of my inhibitions and have fun. I started the year vowing I would go wild. Unfortunately, I sort of suck at it."

Caliph tilted his head and studied her face. He had a way of looking at her that made her feel like he could see straight through her. "Think of it like this, Jen. You're a blank canvas. Beautiful, clean, white. The colors are all there inside you. You just need to set them free."

She swallowed heavily as she glanced at her shoulder. She couldn't see the pretty shades of her tattoo yet, but she knew they were there.

Today she'd taken the first step and grabbed a new beginning. The heaviness that had weighed her down for so long lifted and a spark of joy flared.

Colors.

Set free.

Yeah.

CHAPTER TWO

Caliph leaned back and admired his work. After Jennifer explained the daisy, their conversation slowly faded away as he lost himself in the art. He'd taken his time with this tat, putting special care into every single line. The design was simple, honest, elegant. It reminded him of the woman lying in front of him, the beauty who was going to wear his art for the rest of her life.

He was always flattered, even a little humbled, by the people who put so much faith in his abilities that they allowed him to draw on their skin with permanent ink. It was a gift countless clients had given him even though he'd never admitted such to them.

Jennifer was different from the usual Midnight Ink clientele. She didn't want the tattoo to hide past scars. Many people—male and female—used body art to conceal terrible wounds, physical and emotional. Caliph understood their reasons, felt their pain, and always prayed his art would somehow help them find peace again.

Neither was she trying to draw attention to herself, to appear tough or in-your-face or cool, which, sadly, seemed to be the reason for getting a tat amongst a lot of the younger clients. Caliph suspected Jennifer spent most of her time trying to blend into the background. Which meant her trip to his chair had taken a great deal of courage on her part.

No. Jennifer wasn't trying to hide from her pain or make a big flashy statement. Instead she was incorporating her past failures into the picture, including them as a part of the canvas in an effort to make her stronger, smarter.

He thought about her ex-husband. He had the insane urge to find the asshole and beat him to a pulp for the way he'd damaged Jennifer's self-esteem. It was clear she was a compassionate woman and it pissed him off to see her feeling badly about herself. While she put up a tough front, pain still lingered in her eyes. Her trusting nature as well as her faith in herself had been shaken. Hard.

"You like jazz?" he asked.

She grinned. "Isn't that sort of a prerequisite for living in New Orleans?"

Caliph chuckled. "I know plenty of people who hate it. Tasteless bastards. You ever heard of the Jazz Parlor?"

"In the French Quarter?"

"Yeah. There's a guy playing there Friday night, Jeremy 'Trombone' Lionel."

"Let me guess. He plays the trombone."

Caliph rolled his eyes. "He's one of the best I've ever heard. You wanna go?"

"With you?" Jennifer winced as soon as the question passed her lips. It was an endearing expression that he was starting to become accustomed to. Her mouth seemed to kick in before her brain at times, treating him to her real thoughts. It was refreshing, nice. With Jennifer, you got what you saw. That wasn't true of most women and he found he preferred the unfiltered view.

"Sassy is coming and my brother, Justin, too. So you don't have to worry about me putting the moves on you." For a second he thought he saw a flash of disappointment in her pretty blue eyes. The look encouraged him to add, "Much."

Her smile reflected pure, genuine happiness and Caliph struggled to catch his breath. Something strange stirred in his gut. It was like he'd been sucker punched, but he didn't feel like hitting back.

"I'd love to go. Thank you for the invitation. Should I just meet you here? Friday night?"

He nodded slowly, pleased by her quick response. She didn't employ any of those female games where she had to pretend to think about it so as not to appear too anxious. Jennifer didn't even try to hide the fact she was excited. "Yeah. Eight o'clock work for you?"

"Yep. It sure does." She was still lying on the table, though he'd put the tattoo gun down, his work finished. She bit her lower lip nervously. "Can I look at it now?"

Caliph had been purposely stalling. Not that he thought the tattoo looked bad. In his opinion, it was some of his best work. Knowing what the flower represented to Jennifer had encouraged him to enhance the original drawing, making sure the image would allow her to find that strength and love she was seeking.

"Of course you can." He placed a firm hand on her arm, not mistaking the slight shudder his touch provoked. It wasn't the first time he'd felt her tremble under his fingers. At first, he'd blamed it on fear—he was used to women's frightened responses to him, he was no pretty boy and he knew it—but Jennifer's trusting eyes and flushed face made him wonder if her response was based on something far different.

His stomach clenched again and this time he recognized the cause. Lust. Pure. Unbridled. His cock thickened slightly despite his attempts to will it away with deep, steadying breaths.

Jennifer sat up slowly, hastily tugging up her tube top. Her modesty was cute. It made Caliph want to peel her clothing away slowly, revealing one creamy inch of skin at a time. Her body was sumptuous, though he suspected she probably considered herself fat. Society had done a real number on women with curves in the last fifty years, trying to convince them that stick figures were desirable. Fuck that. As far as he was concerned, Jennifer's generous hourglass was the standard for true feminine beauty.

She followed as he led her to the large mirror hanging against the back wall. He placed a handheld mirror in her hands, watching nervously as she studied the reflection.

"You didn't bleed very much. I have an A and D ointment here that I'll put on before I cover it. Sassy has flyers on her desk that will give you instructions for aftercare. I want you to follow them to the letter." Caliph stuck his hands in the back pockets of his jeans and forced himself to stop rambling. Her silence made him nervous. Christ. He never got this worked up over a client's reaction to a tat. According to Shep, he had more than his fair share of cockiness when it came to his work. Unfortunately that confidence was on shaky ground at the moment.

Finally, he couldn't stand it anymore. "Jen?"

She looked at him—that was when he noticed the tears in her eyes. Oh hell, did she hate it? He'd seen clients cry before, overwhelmed by their first tattoo. But he couldn't stand the thought that maybe she was genuinely upset.

He took the mirror from her and placed it on the counter, then he grasped her hands and gave them a squeeze. "Aw, hell, honey. I'm sorry."

She shook her head. "No. Don't be. It's just—"

"You were nervous about the tat. Second-guessing your decision. I should have told you to go home and sleep on it."

"No." Her grip on his hands tightened. "I love it."

He studied her face, trying to decide if she was lying just to assuage his guilty conscience. As always, he saw nothing but honesty in her gaze. "You do?"

She gave him a wobbly smile, her tears overflowing. "Oh my God, yes. It's even better than I imagined. It's perfect."

Caliph rubbed his jaw, relief suffusing him. "Damn, girl. You scared the shit out of me."

Jennifer laughed, then picked up the mirror once more, taking even longer to admire her new look. The pleasure in her eyes warmed him.

Shep walked over to join them, studying the tat. "Nice work, Cal. That's a beaut."

Caliph nodded, barely acknowledging Shep's compliment. He was more interested in watching Jennifer.

Then he heard Shep mutter something like "aw jeez, here we go" and Caliph's attention turned back to his friend. "What?"

Shep rolled his eyes at Caliph's confusion, then looked at Jennifer. "Congratulations. It's a great tattoo."

Jennifer smiled widely. "Thanks."

Shep returned to his chair as Caliph led Jennifer back to his. Obviously Caliph hadn't managed to mask his attraction to Jennifer from his friend. One of the dangers of working with the same people for so long. The artists in the shop spent too much damn time together. Sometimes it was nice to have such fierce friends at his back, but most of the time it was a pain in the ass. Shep was definitely going to give him shit for this, tease him about getting the hots for the quiet, conservative hotel manager.

Caliph picked up a tube of ointment and turned Jennifer away from him. As he squeezed some onto a stick, he felt her quiver and he had to resist the impulse to lean forward and place a kiss on the back of her slim neck. He spread the lotion onto her skin.

While he worked, he briefly ran through a mental list of reasons why he shouldn't start an affair with Jennifer.

For one thing, the pain from her divorce was present and though she had a good attitude in regards to moving on, she still had a ways to go. Besides, he wasn't looking for a relationship and certainly didn't want to end up hurting her like her ex had.

They were also different people. Jennifer was clearly conservative, reserved. He wasn't sure how she'd respond to his impulsiveness, his tendency to live in the moment. Jennifer didn't strike him as someone who'd find that an easy thing to deal with even for the short-term.

He also wasn't sure what she'd make of their age difference—he was thirty-two to her nearly forty. While she didn't seem hung up on the numbers, Caliph didn't know how she'd feel about sleeping with a younger man. Then, he dismissed that thought as unimportant.

Because there was one way in which she was definitely wrong for him. She may have been married for seventeen years, but he had no doubt her adventures in the bedroom didn't extend much beyond missionary.

Compared to him, she was an innocent.

Caliph couldn't remember the last time he'd had missionary sex. His desires ran along a much different path. He pictured taking Jennifer to the Bastille, a local sex club. He liked the idea of exposing her to that world to see if his suspicions about her sexually submissive nature were true. Her blushes and trembles when he touched her, the way her eyes lowered whenever he asked her to do something, the tiny ways she deferred to him, all combined together in such a way that had him longing to tie her to his bed and fuck her senseless.

Then he imagined Jennifer taking one look at the dark, intimidating sex club with its St. Andrew's crosses and wooden posts with eyebolts and chains. She'd most likely scream as she ran from the room.

Or would she?

Her mention of a safe word earlier threw him. Made him wonder.

And want.

He covered her tattoo with plastic wrap, then he reached for the blouse she'd worn to the shop. He helped put it on, pleased when she turned to face him, allowing him to button it for her.

His excuses for avoiding sex with her fled the instant her pretty blue eyes met his. Jennifer may have been hurt by her ex, but the asshole's cruelty hadn't killed her spirit. The same desire he felt was reflected in her face. Jesus. She wanted him.

"Thanks," she said softly when he'd fastened the last button.

He didn't release the material. He heard Shep talking to his client, a regular, neither man paying attention to them. Sassy had returned from running errands an hour ago and was in the back room. No one else was working yet, the other artists choosing to work later shifts.

Jennifer held his gaze. "Caliph?" she whispered when the silence continued a beat too long.

"How wild do you want to go?"

She frowned, then gave him a rueful grin. "I love my tattoo more than I can say, but I'm definitely not ready for another."

He shook his head. "That's not what I mean." He lowered his voice. "I'm attracted to you, Jen."

She licked her lips, the action a perfect blend of nervousness and arousal. Caliph's cock thickened even more.

"I want you too." Her admission came out more air than tone, but he heard it, let the beauty of it soak deep.

"Friday night, after the jazz club." He didn't say more. He didn't need to. Jennifer was already nodding.

"Okay. I'd like that."

"So would I."

Then her brow furrowed. That didn't take long. Less than five seconds in and she was already reconsidering.

"Tell me what you're thinking," he prodded.

"I've never had a one-night stand."

Caliph was touched by her honesty, but bothered by it as well. That list of reasons he should have stayed away rained down on him again. Women like her didn't do casual sex, but he was pretty damn sure that was all he had to give her. He hadn't lied about his disinterest in marriage. "Jennifer—"

He started to offer her an out, but she cut him off.

"No. I'm not saying that's a bad thing. It's actually a really good thing. I might be putting the pieces back together, Caliph, but the truth of it is, I'm still pretty broken. At this point in my life, I have basically nothing, but sex to give you. Besides, something tells me you'd be a great guy to go wild with."

He grinned. "I'm glad you have such faith in my abilities. I'll do my best not to disappoint you."

She laughed. "I'm not worried."

Caliph knew he should take her agreement to sleep with him and run with it, but he couldn't lie to her when she looked at him with those gorgeous, trusting eyes. She needed to know exactly what she was agreeing to.

"Maybe you should be. Because, Jen, you *will* need a safe word Friday night."

Her cheeks flushed a pretty pink, but she held her ground. His respect for her went up several more notches.

"Does it make me sound completely twisted if I say that's the hottest thing anyone's ever said to me?"

He barked out a laugh and shook his head. "You're a fascinating woman, Jen. And I can't wait to paint on your canvas some more."

CHAPTER THREE

Jennifer leaned back in her chair and wished the soft, mellow music would work its magic on her. As it was, she was a bundle of nerves and pent-up hormones. Ever since Caliph issued his invitation to the club—and everything that would come after—she'd found it impossible to think about anything else. Her work was suffering. She hadn't slept more than a few hours each night and the woman who never missed a meal was suddenly living on only a couple of bites here and there.

In a word, she was a mess.

Caliph reached under the table and placed a firm hand on her knee to still her rapidly bouncing leg.

She glanced at him. "Sorry," she whispered.

When they'd entered the club, Caliph had escorted her to a table along a side wall. He'd wasted no time pulling his chair as close to hers as possible. Sassy had come with them, but within minutes of arriving, she'd run into other friends. Jennifer glanced over to the bar and saw the vivacious woman laughing and talking. Jennifer wished she felt even half as carefree at the moment.

Caliph squeezed her knee gently. "Relax, Jen."

It was on the tip of her tongue to tell him that was easier said than done, but before she could speak, a man approached their table.

"There you are. Sorry I'm late, Cal. Fucking work is insane right now. We landed three big clients, so I'm in deadline hell." The man plopped into a chair across from them. "Hey. You must be Jennifer. I'm Justin."

Jennifer took the man's outstretched hand and shook it. "Nice to meet you."

Caliph pushed the extra Guinness he'd ordered toward his brother. "Here. Had the waitress bring this over when you texted to say you were on your way. Figured you could use a cold one."

Justin smiled and muttered a quick word of thanks before taking a drink.

Jennifer was struck by how different the men were. Where Caliph was a huge, hulking figure with his smooth, shaved head, tattooed skin and tight black T-shirt, Justin was long, lean and clean-cut with an expensive hairstyle, conservative shirt and new jeans. Caliph was linebacker to his brother's point guard, and besides their height, she was hard-pressed to find one physical similarity between them.

Caliph must have noticed her attempt. "Don't bother trying. Justin's my half-brother and, according to our mom, he's the spitting image of his old man, while I'm the mirror image of mine."

Justin chuckled. "Pisses her off too. Says it's not fair that none of her kids got even a speck of her good looks."

They all laughed.

"I can't decide if I want to meet your mother or not. She seems like a force to be reckoned with," Jennifer joked.

Caliph put his arm around her shoulder, the close proximity doing funny things to her libido. Jennifer struggled to keep cool, but had no doubt her flushed face was giving her away to both men at the table. "Don't worry, Jen. I'd protect you from her."

Justin snorted. "Yeah right. Just admit you're afraid of her too. Hell, we all are. When Meg Lewis says move, you better believe everybody in the house goes into motion."

"Everybody? You have other brothers and sisters?" As she asked the question, she realized how little she really knew about Caliph. This was only the third time she'd even seen the man and she'd agreed to have sex with him. Responsible Jennifer would never have dreamed of jumping into bed with a stranger, yet the decision to sleep with Caliph had been surprisingly easy. And it occurred to her that most of her nervousness wasn't based on fear, but anticipation.

"My mom had four kids, Justin's the oldest, then me, then our brother Jett. Chloe is the only girl and the baby."

"Which means she's spoiled rotten," Justin added.

Jennifer could tell from their expressions both men adored their kid sister.

Caliph ran his finger along the nape of her neck and Jennifer resisted the urge to shudder…and purr. "But the family is actually bigger than that."

Justin took a swig of beer and put the glass back down. "Mom has taken in a lot of foster kids over the years. She was a social worker before she got married. After she started having kids, she quit her job."

"Her workdays were unbelievably long and she didn't want to be away from us for so many hours every day," Caliph continued. "Of course, she also couldn't stand the thought of other kids out there who needed a safe place to stay."

"Over the years, we've had six foster brothers and sisters live with us, off and on, depending on how much the system wanted to fuck with them." Justin's tone didn't mask his disgust and Caliph's expression proved he felt the same way.

She could imagine how hard it would be to bring a child into your home only to have the courts yank them back out to return them somewhere less safe. Jennifer smiled sympathetically. "Your mom sounds great. What about your dad…or sorry, dads?"

Justin chuckled. "I was an oops during my parents' senior year at college. They never got married, but I know my dad. He's still around. Papa Lewis is the one she married."

"My dad was a boxer before he started working on oil rigs. He wasn't home much. Used to joke that was why my mom kept taking in strays. To keep from getting lonely."

"As if you could get lonely in that house," Justin added.

Caliph's eyes dimmed. "Dad had a massive heart attack a few years ago and died."

Jennifer took Caliph's hands. "Oh. I'm so sorry."

Caliph squeezed her fingers lightly, clearly appreciating her words. "It's okay, but thanks."

Justin's cell beeped and he glanced at the screen, his eyes going wide with excitement. "Hot damn."

Caliph shook his head in feigned disapproval. "Let me guess. Ned?"

Justin gave his brother a shit-eating grin. "Yep. Turns out my partner may have an interesting, er, prospect for us tonight. You guys care if I shove off early?"

Caliph pointed to Justin's glass. "You're leaving money for that beer. I'm getting sick of covering your bar tabs whenever you get a better offer."

Justin threw a ten-dollar bill on the table with a laugh. "Nice to meet you, Jennifer."

"You too," she said as he walked away. She turned to look at Caliph. "Prospect?"

Caliph hesitated for a moment. Finally, he answered. "My brother and his marketing partner, Ned, are best friends. They like to share."

The light went on. "Women?"

He nodded. "Yeah." He studied her face as she fought to school her features. She certainly didn't want to look like a judgmental prude when the truth was the whole idea made her hot.

"Oh. Well, that's cool."

Caliph laughed. "Glad you think so."

His words ran over her like ice water and for the first time since she'd agreed to sleep with him, panic set in. "I mean, I don't, I didn't—"

Caliph took her hands in his once more. "Relax, Jen. Tonight is just you and me. Threesomes are Justin's kink. Not mine."

"What are yours?" The question fell out before she could think better of it, but she didn't bother to take it back. Despite her undeniable horniness, she hadn't taken complete leave of her senses. Probably best to put all their cards on the table now.

"Bondage. Domination. Spanking. Wax play. Anal."

He rattled off his grocery list of sex acts with such ease Jennifer struggled to catch her breath. "Oh. Is that all?"

Caliph laughed at her joke, shaking his head. "You're adorable." He wrapped his arm around her shoulder and pulled her closer. His size became even more apparent as she was engulfed in sheer muscle. "Tonight's not about my kinks, Jen. You wanted to go wild. Tell me how."

She licked her suddenly dry lips. She'd read about—fantasized over—everything he'd mentioned. But there was safety in fiction. Caliph was offering to make her dreams a reality and that scared the shit out of her. "I sort of thought I was pushing the envelope by having sex with a virtual stranger. Starting to think I might be out of my league."

Caliph ran the back of one finger along her cheek in a way that should have been endearing, but was the equivalent of throwing gasoline on a flame. Her pussy clenched. "Your league is just fine. Tell me where you see tonight going."

She considered his list. "I don't know you well enough to let you tie me up and render me helpless."

Caliph grinned. "Good girl. You're right. You don't."

He accepted her admission too easily and she was concerned he'd misunderstood. "But…that doesn't mean I don't want it. I mean…I would…eventually."

Heat suffused her face. God. Caliph had invited her out tonight—only offered her one evening. She hadn't meant to insinuate she wanted more.

He cupped her cheeks in his hands, forcing her to look at him. "I love your expressions."

She frowned. "What do you—"

"You're a very easy woman to read, Jen. I want tonight to go well. And if it does, we can talk about seeing each other again. There's nothing to say a one-night stand can't run over into two. You seem to be a very sensual woman with some fantasies that need exploring. Let's just roll with it. Don't shield your words or hide your feelings from me because they aren't going to scare me away."

Jennifer wasn't sure how to respond. She'd come here tonight fully prepared for a one-night stand. Truthfully that seemed like the most she could handle. She'd never mastered casual sex. Ever since she'd lost her virginity in eleventh grade, she'd had a tendency to lead with her heart. If she let tonight trickle into more, wouldn't she be setting herself up for heartache?

After nursing a broken heart for the better part of last year, she wasn't sure she was ready to open herself up for more hurt.

"Uh oh. You're thinking too much." He stood, throwing money on the table. "Come on, gorgeous. I'm taking you back to my place and fucking you until you forget your name."

She rose slowly, then hesitated for a moment. She hadn't lied earlier about what made this night seem wild, even if it felt tame compared to Caliph's sexual proclivities. Essentially, they really were strangers. She didn't even know where he lived. This was stupid and reckless.

Caliph held out his hand. "Give me your phone."

"Why?" Even as she asked the question, she handed it over.

"Who's your best friend?"

"Beth."

He turned it on and clicked on her list of contacts before handing it back to her. "Send a text to Beth. Tell her where you're going and give her my address."

"Okay." Apparently Jennifer wasn't the only one with common sense. Caliph read her concerns and he'd found a way to alleviate the fear. She tapped out the address he gave, promising to check in, and then she hit send. No doubt Beth would be beating on her apartment door first thing tomorrow morning, excitedly demanding details and a complete recap of the evening.

"Better?" he asked.

She nodded.

"You still wanna come home with me?"

She smiled and released a long, slow breath. "So damn much."

Caliph stopped by the bar to make sure Sassy had a ride home. They'd decided to leave her car at Midnight Ink and ride to the club together. He assured her that her car would be fine at the tattoo shop overnight, so he drove her to his house. The trip was surprisingly relaxing as they talked about anything and everything—her family, his work at the shop, their mutual love of jazz. When they reached his house, Caliph turned the car off, but neither of them bothered to get out. They just kept talking.

Though they'd only known each other a short time, Jennifer felt like she'd shared more of herself with Caliph in just one evening than she had with Marcus during the last few years of their marriage.

Finally, Caliph glanced at his phone, his eyebrows rising. "Damn. Where did that time go?" Nearly two hours had passed, but to Jennifer it felt like the blink of an eye.

"I have no idea, but Caliph…" Her nervousness had evaporated somewhere in the midst of their long talk, and now, when faced with the prospect of going inside, she felt nothing but overwhelming desire and need.

He'd said her expressions gave her away. Apparently he hadn't lied. Caliph's eyes darkened with honest-to-God hunger. It took her breath away. No one had ever looked at her with such unbridled lust.

"I don't think I'm going to make it inside," she whispered, assaulted by an arousal so painful and beautiful she wasn't sure she could walk without coming.

"Oh fuck yeah." Caliph was out of the car and

opening her door between one blink of the eye and the next. He reached down to help her out, wrapping her in his huge embrace. She recalled building a tent as a child, tying the corners of a big blanket to the four posts of her bed. She'd huddle beneath it in the darkness, soaking up the warmth and security of her snug hiding spot. Caliph's hug reminded her of that place, bringing back sensations of being safe and happy.

Neither of them spoke when he loosened his grip, taking her hand to lead her into his small house. It reminded her of the man—simple, straightforward. His yard was neatly trimmed, the porch clean, freshly painted. When he opened the door and turned on the light, she admired the cozy warmth of his home. Family portraits covered the wall of his living room.

"Want a tour?" he offered.

She shook her head. There would be time for that later. Maybe. "No." She let that one word tell him exactly what she wanted.

Caliph tightened his grip on her hand and tugged her down a narrow hallway and straight into his bedroom.

"Take off your clothes."

The quick demand would have freaked out old Jennifer, but the woman Caliph was helping her discover was beyond modesty.

She unbuttoned her blouse, shrugging it over her shoulders without hesitance. Caliph didn't join her in disrobing. Instead he ate her alive with his eyes, and amazingly, he appeared to like what he saw. Marcus had pointed out the fact that she'd let herself go, that she'd gained a few pounds, as yet another reason he'd wanted out. She shoved that memory away. The bastard had no place here tonight. She wasn't going to let him cast his miserable shadow on one minute of this.

Jennifer toed off her shoes, then unzipped her skirt. Her actions slowed. Despite her attempts to hold on to her newfound confidence, she found it wavering.

Caliph stepped closer. "You're beautiful. Perfect. Take off the skirt."

She reacted without thought—as the skirt, her panties, and even her bra fell away with ease—until she stood before him completely naked. Jennifer resisted the urge to close her eyes, to hide before she could see his response. She wasn't thin and she sure as hell wasn't young.

"Turn around," Caliph demanded.

Since entering the room, she'd noticed the change in his demeanor. Her gentle giant had disappeared, replaced by this commanding, sexy-as-sin man. Every order he issued sent shivers of excitement down her spine.

Jennifer spun a half turn, then paused, letting him look his fill. Facing away from him gave her the freedom to relax, to stop working overtime to shield her expressions. She scrunched her eyes closed tightly and prayed.

Please don't let him be disgusted like Marcus. Please.

She jerked slightly when Caliph's hands landed on her shoulders. "Dammit, Jen. Stop that."

Her eyelids flew open and that was when she noticed the mirror in front of her. So much for playing it cool.

She captured his gaze in the reflection, forced herself to face what she'd been afraid to see.

"What were you thinking about?"

She didn't bother to lie. "Marcus. He didn't care for my looks."

His fingers stroked her shoulders, drawing circles on her skin. "He doesn't have any place here. He was an idiot and a fool. His loss. My gain."

She smiled, swallowing hard against the lump in her throat, fighting to hold back the tears threatening to fall. God. She'd told him she was broken. Falling apart and crying like a baby in his arms would only drive that point home.

She wouldn't do it. Jennifer took a deep breath, then turned around to face him. "Do I get to see you naked?"

He cupped her cheeks and placed a soft kiss on her lips. Their first kiss. Like everything about him, it washed away her preconceived notions of how a man who looked like Caliph would kiss. It was soft and warm, nothing scary or rough.

"Go sit on the bed."

More commands. When she considered their conversations—few though there had been—she realized almost everything he'd ever asked of her had been worded as a demand, rather than a request. And yet that didn't bother her. Didn't send her hackles up like it would whenever Marcus tried to tell her what to do.

In fact, Caliph's orders made her hot, made her melt inside. She walked over to his bed, sitting on the edge to watch as he treated her to her own private striptease.

Once Caliph removed his shirt, Jennifer was able to finally see the whole picture of his tattoos, rather than the half peeks she'd glimpsed at the shop and tonight.

"Wow," she whispered, rising from the bed. She walked over, compelled to add touch to sight. She ran her fingers over every beautiful work of art on his chest, his arms. Stepping around him, she stroked the large tree that covered his back, her eyes discovering the clever way he'd incorporated the names of his brothers and sisters into the branches and leaves. It reinforced what she'd learned at the jazz club earlier. Family was very important to him. That thought touched her.

Her grandmother had always told her when she was younger to look at how a man treated his mother because that offered a clue about how he would treat his wife. Figures that pearl of wisdom reappeared now—two decades too late. Marcus barely spoke to his mother. Then she considered what a shame it was that Caliph didn't believe in marriage. Given his undeniable love for his mother, she suspected he'd shower a wife in adoration.

"You've gone quiet back there." Caliph's deep voice drew her from her thoughts.

"Just admiring the artwork. It's amazing."

He turned to look at her, smiling. "I was worried it might be a bit too much for you."

She shook her head. For old Jennifer, yeah. The image of so much ink would have intimidated and freaked her out a bit. Triggered all those stupid stereotypes she suddenly hated. Now she wasn't sure she'd ever seen anything more beautiful. "Not at all."

"Good. Then I'm going for broke." He slid off his shoes, unzipped his jeans and dropped them to the floor. Caliph went commando.

Her gaze drifted lower. Her subconscious acknowledged the tats on his legs, but Caliph's fully erect cock overshadowed them.

"Whoa."

Caliph chuckled, taking her hand and wrapping it around his thick girth. He kept his grip on hers as he guided her strokes along his hard flesh.

"How long has it been?"

She searched for an answer, trying to calculate months…and then years. Finally, she said, "Too long."

"Don't move." He stepped away from her, quickly

pulling a drop cloth from under his bed. She watched as he stripped away the soft comforter, replacing it with the cloth.

"Are we painting or something?" she asked.

He looked over his shoulder at her and winked. "Oh yeah. Art class is about to begin." He returned to her and kissed her briefly once more.

"Go lie on the bed. On your back."

Moment of truth. Thank God.

She assumed the position, expecting Caliph to join her, to crawl over her body and give her exactly what she'd been longing for.

Instead, he walked away from the bed, dragging a box from the closet.

She started to ask what he was doing, but something about his demeanor told her to remain silent. Again, she was struck by his dominance, his complete control over his body and tonight's adventure. He was clearly ready to roll if his hard-on was anything to go by.

Jennifer was very familiar with the wham-bam-thank-you-ma'am style of sex. It had been Marcus' forte, but Caliph didn't appear to be in a hurry to do the deed. Instead, he was drawing out the experience, ramping up her desires with anticipation. It was a deadly concept. And freaking hot.

After years of lackluster, predictable sex, the appeal

of not knowing what was going to happen was cranking up her arousal, making it hard for her not to find her clit with her own fingers to grant herself some measure of relief.

Caliph approached the bed. "I said I wouldn't tie you up and I won't. But I need you to lie perfectly still, Jen. Keep your arms and legs where I put them without moving. Can you do that?"

She had no idea, but she damn well intended to try. She nodded.

"Your safe word is daisy."

It was perfect. He'd picked the one word that would remind her she was in control. That she was strong.

"Daisy," she repeated, blinking once more against the tears forming. God. She wasn't sad, wasn't scared, yet she felt the uncontrollable urge to crawl into a ball and cry her heart out. What was wrong with her? She was exactly where she wanted to be, doing something she'd never dreamed she'd have the courage to try.

Hello basket case.

Caliph reached into the box and pulled out a candle. She ran through his list of kinks. Wax play. She'd read about it. Knew the hot wax would hurt, but that pain could morph into something even hotter inside. She wanted to experience it and she had no doubt Caliph could make it good for her.

He didn't pause in his preparations as he removed several different colored candles from the box, then a lighter. He set them up on his nightstand, lighting each one. Once he was ready, he tossed the empty box in a corner and turned back to her.

He leaned over the bed, one of his knees landing on the mattress by her hip. Lifting her arms, he placed her hands beside her head on the pillow. The position was one of pure surrender. Her heart raced as fear, anticipation, and need all morphed together until it took every ounce of strength in her body not to pull Caliph on top of her and force him inside her.

"I'm not sure I can do this."

Caliph frowned, concern in his dark brown eyes. "If it's too much, too painful—"

"No, it's not that. I'm so fucking horny. I don't think I can wait."

His face cleared, replaced with a grin so genuine and mischievous, she knew she'd just sealed her own fate. Caliph was going to drag this out, there was no denying it. He'd play with her until she begged and even then, she suspected he wouldn't give in.

"You're not going to take it easy on me, are you?" she asked.

He shook his head as he moved lower on the mattress. "No." He grasped her knees and pulled her legs apart. "I'm not."

She glanced down and saw her ankles were lined up perfectly with the bottom posts on his bed. Part of her was sorry she'd taken bondage off the table. If it turned out tonight was all she got, she'd regret missing out on that experience.

Maybe a compromise.

"Could you tie just my legs?" With her hands free, she could still escape the bonds, though she knew she wouldn't try.

Caliph studied her face, not bothering to hide his pleasure at her request. "Are you sure?"

She nodded. "Please."

He reached toward the foot of the bed, pulling up straps that had been tucked beneath the mattress.

"Seriously?" she asked when she realized the ties were already secured to the poles.

"Never claimed to be a choirboy."

She let her gaze travel over his chest and erection. "Believe me, that thought never entered my mind."

He tickled the bottom of her feet as he strapped her ankles to the bed. She was grateful for the reason to giggle, otherwise sheer panic would have taken over.

Once she was tied in place, he crawled over her body, remaining above her on all fours. "Okay?"

"Yeah."

"Say your word and the straps come off."

She shook her head. "No. I don't want to say it. I trust you."

He gave her a crooked grin, then bent to kiss her. This time, the kid gloves came off. His lips pressed against hers roughly, his tongue seeking entrance to her mouth. She opened and returned the kiss.

Twice she started to lift her hands from the pillow, wanting to wrap them around his neck, to hold him tight to her. Both times, Caliph issued a warning growl. The deep timbre of his voice made her wet and hot and achy. The kiss was intense. Primal. Passionate.

He broke off the connection to kneel on the bed, reaching for a bottle of mineral oil. He squirted some on his hands, then began to rub it into her skin. The sexy massage did little to relax her. Instead, it had the opposite effect, firing off a whole new set of needs. Every part of her body was awake, alert, aware. Aroused. She felt as if she was coming unhinged as her pussy clenched continually, seeking penetration.

After several minutes—that seemed like years—he lifted his hands. "Ready to get started?"

She snorted. "Dear God. What have we been doing the past half hour?"

"Preliminaries. Prepping the area. Getting ready to add the design, then the color."

Tattoo-speak. Before her turn in his chair on Tuesday, she wouldn't have understood the allusion. "So now what? You draw?"

He nodded. "Yep. Time for some art."

He rose from the bed, strode across the room to turn off the overhead light, then returned and lifted one of the lit candles. "How much do you know about wax play?"

"Next to nothing."

He looked at her face and she wondered what he saw there. "You want a brief lesson? Wanna know about the wax, temperatures, stuff like that?"

"Nope. Don't give a shit. For the first time in my life, I think I'd prefer experience over education."

"Yeah. That sealed it. Your one-night stand just became a weekend. You up for it?"

She laughed quietly. "Guess it all depends on how you stick the landing."

"Is that right?" Caliph cut her laugh short when he tilted the candle, allowing a large splash of wax to hit her nipple.

"Fuck." She lifted her hands, intent on wiping the painful substance away, but Caliph narrowed his eyes in warning.

Slowly, she forced them back to the pillow. "I think it would be easier if my hands were bound too."

Caliph moved the candle over to her other breast. Jennifer sucked in a deep breath and held it, preparing herself. His second splash of hot liquid hit its mark as well, coating her nipple in white. She clenched her fists, but kept her hands in place.

"I would have thought you'd realized I'm not going for easy, Jen. This weekend is all about pushing your limits, driving you wild."

It was poised on the tip of her tongue to call him a bastard when he placed another large splash of the red-hot liquid on her stomach.

And as usual, he read the thought. "Careful, gorgeous. It's never a good idea to taunt a man who's bigger than you."

He put the white candle back on his nightstand and picked up a blue one. After that, all conversation died as Jennifer gave herself up to the moment.

Each splash of wax burned, scorching a path through her skin straight to her pussy. She clenched her inner muscles, though they remained empty, aching. Caliph ignored her pleas, her cries, her demand that he "put down those goddamn candles and fuck me."

Jennifer lost all sense of time, of place. The dark room, illuminated only by candles, allowed her to disappear into the shadows. After spending the past year standing in a glaring light that forced her to see and acknowledge every flaw and shortcoming, the black night was a blessed relief.

Here, she was sheltered, safe.

She started to anticipate and look forward to each splash, every sting. Her eyelids drifted closed and her begging turned to just one word. His name.

"Caliph. Caliph. Caliph."

Jennifer wasn't sure how long she'd lain on his bed after Caliph stopped painting her body with wax. When she opened her eyes, she was surprised to discover he'd turned on his bedside lamp.

It took several moments for her gaze to focus, for her vision to clear enough to find him. He was sitting on the side of the bed, looking at her body.

When he realized she was looking at him, he smiled. "You're beautiful."

Jennifer lifted her head to glance down. She gasped as she took in his artwork. Her body was a kaleidoscope of texture, shape, and form.

He'd set her colors free.

CHAPTER FOUR

Caliph took his time cleaning the wax from Jennifer's soft skin. He'd indulged in wax play with several women over the years, but none of them had ever responded so naturally, so intensely as Jennifer. She'd accepted his dominance—handing herself over to him, allowing him to take her somewhere she'd never gone before. Her trust was awakening places in him he didn't know existed.

He'd covered her with mineral oil in order to make the clean up easier. Once the last of the wax was stripped from her body, he placed the blunt knife he'd been using on the nightstand.

Jennifer's eyes were closed, not in exhaustion, but bliss. Her chest rose and fell rapidly and her nipples were tight, hard little cherries begging him to take a bite. He let his hand drift lower, watching her face closely as he dragged his fingers along the slit between her legs from anus to clit.

She gasped, her gaze finding his. She was wet, hot, the scent of her arousal increasing his own hunger.

"I want you, Jen."

She lifted one shoulder, the gesture so innocent and honest it hit him like a wrecking ball. "I'm yours."

He tried to ignore the incredible impact those words had on him. "How far are you willing to go?"

Her eyes blinked rapidly, her brow creased as she considered his question. Then, she smiled. "I'm going to be forty soon, Caliph. I've wasted decades of my life, settling for good enough instead of reaching for something amazing. I'm tired of coloring inside the lines. I want an explosion, an adventure. Hell, I'd even settle for a red-hot mess. I guess what I'm saying is I want as much as you're willing to give me."

Caliph felt lightheaded as he considered her offer. "Be very sure, Jen. If you're serious about this, I'm not going to hold back. I'll make demands that I will expect to be obeyed."

Her face flushed, but there was no mistaking it for nervousness. Right before his eyes, the flower bloomed, the petals opening. She wasn't scared. She was in.

"Daisy." He felt compelled to remind her one last time. "That's the only word that will end this. Not no or ouch or even stop."

"Daisy," she repeated. "I'll remember."

Caliph reached down and released the straps on her ankles. Jennifer made a soft mew of disappointment that made him chuckle. "Don't worry. We'll use those again. Later. Right now…"

He reached for her hand, drawing her up until she was sitting in front of him on the bed. Jennifer used her freedom to press her legs together, not because of modesty, but as a means of seeking relief. He allowed her the brief attempt, perfectly aware it wouldn't help much. She'd been riding the edge of an orgasm for nearly an hour. He longed to say to hell with everything, push her to her back and fuck her until they both went blind with pleasure.

And while that was clearly what she wanted, it wasn't even close to what she needed.

He grasped her hand and tugged gently until she was standing beside the bed.

He took a few minutes to clean up, removing the drop cloth and putting the comforter back on the bed. Then he sat on the edge.

"Kneel here." Caliph threw a pillow on the floor and put her in the position he wanted, Jennifer on her knees between his legs. "Leave your hands on your thighs. Don't move them."

Gripping his cock, he ran his hand along the hard flesh as Jennifer watched. She licked her lips and started to move toward him, but he stopped her with a firm grip on her long brown hair. She gasped at his tight hold.

"Just watch, Jen. Don't do anything I don't tell you to do."

Her breathing became more erratic, but she didn't try to pull away. "Okay."

He continued to stroke his cock, letting her see how hard he liked it, how fast, what places were more sensitive than others. Jennifer was a serious student, her expressive blue eyes observing everything he did.

"Open your mouth."

She obeyed instantly and he was struck by the fact she didn't lift her hands or try to move closer. She simply did as he asked. Caliph touched her lips with the head of his cock, but made no attempt to push inside her mouth.

"Let me feel your tongue."

Again, she gave him what he asked for. Her licks were timid at first, quick swipes, but soon she became more adventurous, taking longer tastes, teasing the opening to his cock with the tip of her tongue. He fought to regulate his own breathing as she treated his dick like an ice cream cone she simply couldn't get enough of.

After several minutes, Caliph used his fist in her hair to tug her away. Jennifer's eyes closed and she moaned softly. She was definitely getting off on his roughness, on his control. It drove the Dom inside him crazy. He wasn't sure he'd ever met such a natural—yet untried—submissive. Every alpha nerve in his body was clamoring to take her, teach her, make her his own.

He shook off the thought. Jennifer wasn't looking for more than the weekend and she wasn't ready for what he was considering.

Shit, he hadn't thought he was looking for a more serious relationship prior to tonight. He was happy with his bachelor status. Or he had been.

Now…

Jennifer moved slightly and he realized she was frowning.

"I'm sorry. Did I do something wrong?"

He shook his head. Her tone of voice, laced with fear of failure, pissed him off. Her fucking ex had a lot to answer for. "No, Jen. You did everything right. I needed a second to get control or this was going to be over too damn quick."

Her face lit up. "Really?"

He rolled his eyes at the disbelief in her question. "Yes. Really. New rule, Jen. No more talking."

She narrowed her eyes briefly.

"You don't like that rule?" he asked.

"What if I have questions?"

He resisted the urge to laugh. She was inquisitive, a newbie to all the things he wanted to expose her to. "Make a list in your head. We'll do a Q and A afterwards."

She giggled, but didn't complain. "Okay."

"Now open that mouth and come here." This time he didn't stop with just the head. He pushed deeper, going slowly to give her time to adjust to his size. He figured he wasn't much bigger than the average guy, but Jennifer clearly wasn't accustomed to giving blowjobs. She struggled a bit.

Once half his cock was in, he paused. "Take more."

Her brow creased, but she made the attempt.

Caliph cupped her cheeks, running his thumbs along the soft skin there. "Open your throat and take me all the way in."

She resisted when he pushed against the back of her throat. His grip on her face tightened.

"You can do it, Jen. Just relax and try."

He thrust in several times more, watching as Jennifer fought to give him what he wanted. Finally, on the sixth attempt, something gave way and his cock slid deeper.

Her eyes widened, first with surprise, then with obvious delight. If Caliph had been able to offer praise, he would have. As it was, it was taking all his powers of concentration not to come too quickly. Now that Jennifer had mastered the technique, she was putting it to good use. Her head bobbed along his flesh, taking him deeper, swallowing at just the right time. Her hands had moved to grip his thighs and she was using them as leverage to help her move even faster.

Jesus. He'd been holding her face as a means of control before, but now he needed his hands there just to fucking hold on.

Twice, three more times, she took him in and Caliph gave up the battle. A deep groan rumbled through his chest as he came. Jennifer was ready, swallowing his come as spots formed behind his eyes.

"Mother of God," he said through gritted teeth. When the last drop had been squeezed out, he tried to pull back, but Jennifer followed him, holding his now-flaccid cock in her mouth as she rested her head against his thigh.

Caliph ran his hands through her long tresses gently as he lightly massaged her scalp.

Then he cupped her cheek and pushed her face away from his cock. She looked up at him and smiled. He started to return the grin, then he noticed her hands were still on his thighs.

"You moved your hands."

Jennifer seemed confused for a few seconds before her memory kicked in. "I forgot."

He frowned, though he was far from angry. She'd just offered him the perfect opportunity to expand their play. "And it appears you forgot that you aren't supposed to speak either."

Jennifer bit her lip, but the excited flush in her cheeks urged him to go on. He'd long ago learned that many women craved the dangerous bad boy. Caliph had no problem playing that role because it allowed him to indulge his own desire to dominate. And punish.

"Stand up, Jen."

She rose, her movements a bit wobbly. Caliph placed a firm hand on her elbow to help.

"I think it's time you learn what happens to subs who don't do as they're told."

She blinked rapidly. "Subs?"

His jaw tightened and she winced, aware she'd spoken out of turn once again. He gripped her wrist and tugged until she lay facedown over his lap.

Jennifer fought briefly against the position, her body going into flight mode before her brain could catch up. He placed a firm hand on her upper back, pressing down, while his other kept her legs from thrashing. Then he paused for a full minute, letting her adjust to the situation and waiting to see if she would say the safe word.

When it became clear she wasn't going to speak, he moved his hand from her legs and began to stroke her bare ass. She jerked at the initial touch, clearly expecting him to strike rather than caress.

"Do you understand why you're being punished?"

Silence met his question.

"You can answer my question, Jen. In fact, I expect you to respond when I ask you something."

"Yes. I know why."

"Tell me."

She shivered slightly. "I disobeyed your orders. Three times."

"That's right. You did." He lifted his hand and brought it down against her ass. Jennifer's response was exactly as he'd anticipated. She reared up, intent on escape. He kept one hand on her back, preventing it. He spanked her several more times, the rhythm of the blows varying in placement and strength. He didn't pause. Jennifer knew how to stop him—her word was there to protect her if she needed it.

Apparently she didn't. Her hands found his right shin, gripping it tightly as he continued her punishment. After a dozen or so swats, he pushed her legs open, running his fingers along her slit.

Jennifer moaned. She was hot, wet and so fucking aroused. He'd kept her on the verge of a climax for nearly two hours.

She tried to push closer to his fingers, seeking more.

"You want to come, Jen?"

"Please," she whispered.

Caliph pushed two fingers inside her pussy, the simple touch triggering an avalanche.

Jennifer reared up roughly as she cried out. "Oh

God. Harder."

Caliph continued to move until she stiffened, her body trembling with her orgasm.

He had glimpsed Jennifer's submissiveness in the shop. When combined with her bruised self-esteem, it had tugged at his heart, triggered a need in him to reach out to hold her.

He longed to expose her desires, to show Jennifer the beauty to be found in giving herself to a man completely, while trying to bolster her confidence. Caliph was pissed off at her ex for the number he'd worked on her and he hoped he never ran into the man on the street. His plan had been to give her one night to discover who she was and exactly how much she had to offer.

What he hadn't expected was to find the perfect complement to his own desires. She was the yin to his yang, the medium to his technique.

But Jennifer wasn't looking for a relationship. She'd said so herself. And he believed her. Understood that she truly needed time to find herself.

Even as he thought the words, he wanted to rage against the cliché.

She began to tremble and he heard her soft sniffle. He lifted her, drawing her onto his lap. Caliph felt a splash of wetness on his skin.

"Jen?"

She burrowed deeper against his chest, obviously ashamed of her tears.

"Hey." Caliph lifted her face until he could see her pretty blue eyes. "Don't hide from me."

"I d-don't know why I'm c-crying. You must think I'm insane."

He frowned. "No. I think you're a beautiful woman who just experienced something new and pretty fucking intense. It's going to take you a little while to find your footing again. Just hold tight to me, okay? I won't let you fall."

Her grip around his neck tightened, her tears flowing more freely now. He placed soft kisses on the top of her head, whispering "shh" over and over until her trembling stopped and her breathing slowed. Her response to his spanking was normal. She was new to the experience and though there was genuine submissiveness at her core, it was natural for her to be confused by her response and her feelings about the act, as they were likely in direct opposition to everything she'd ever been raised to believe about being an independent woman.

"Feel better?"

She nodded. "I didn't expect—" She paused and he sensed she was searching for a way to explain.

"You loved it."

It wasn't a question. Her responses to him were incredible, open, honest. Just like the woman in his arms.

"So much," she whispered.

"You want more?"

"God yes."

Caliph's cock had begun to thicken during the spanking. There was something wholly arousing about watching a woman's beautiful ass turn red under his hand. But Jennifer's request, her desire for something stronger, fed his needs.

He pushed her onto her stomach on the bed, lifting her hips until her knees found support on the edge of the mattress. He stood behind her, stroking her ass for only a moment.

Caliph reached for the nightstand and donned a condom. "How hard do you want it, Jen?"

She shuddered, her body quivering in response. Obviously the spanking had awakened something inside her. Pain turned her on.

"Please, Caliph. I need—"

Her tone told him all he needed to know. Before she could finish her request, he was there, shoving in to the hilt in one strong, deep blow.

Jennifer screamed as her inner muscles clenched around his cock. Caliph didn't give way, didn't ease up. Instead he pummeled faster.

Her first orgasm hit hard and fast, but he wasn't

finished yet. He couldn't give up the heaven he found inside her body. She didn't shy away from his strength, from his rough claiming. Instead, she added to the pressure, her fists gripping the bedspread as she shoved back in time with his thrusts forward.

Caliph's vision blurred as his balls drew tight. Usually he had more self-control than this. He tried to draw in a deep breath, fighting against the desire to come. It was all happening too fast.

Jennifer needed—deserved—so much more. He forced himself to slow his pace.

"No." Jennifer sensed his retreat, so she doubled her efforts, pushing against him more roughly.

He gripped her hips, attempting to hold her still. She didn't give up the struggle to take control.

"Jen. Stop." His voice was deep, stern. Demanding.

She responded to it instantly.

"Caliph," she whispered. "Please."

Her soft plea was almost his undoing. Almost.

Then he shook his head. She was topping from the bottom. He'd never let a sub get away with that. Ever.

He slapped her ass, two hard blows to remind her who was in charge.

The effort was wasted on his sexy lover. Rather than subdue her, it fired her libido even more.

She lifted her ass higher. "Again. Do it again."

He stifled the laugh clamoring for release. His submissive was going to be fun to tame. Caliph pulled out and stepped away from the bed.

Jennifer lifted her head, looking over her shoulder. She started to speak, but he shook his head once, the only warning he intended to give her.

She closed her mouth and waited, though he could see how difficult the effort was.

"Roll over onto your back. Open your legs and hold them that way until I tell you otherwise."

It was time to test some limits. Jennifer had come to his bed with the desire to expand her sexual experiences. While there was no denying she enjoyed the blowjob and doggie style, neither were likely new for her. She'd responded strongly to the unknown—the wax play and the spanking—and he was anxious to introduce her to more.

Jennifer slowly spread her legs, gripping them below the knee. He could tell she was uneasy with being on display. Despite all they'd already done, lying still while exposing her most private places was going to force her to overcome her issues with self-esteem.

Caliph didn't bother to mask his perusal of her body. He let his gaze slide over every sensuous curve. He wondered if she'd be willing to pose for him some time. Let him draw her. Her body was art incarnate—a beautiful study.

Once he'd looked his fill, he decided to up the ante.

"Touch yourself."

CHAPTER FIVE

Heat suffused Jennifer's body at the idea of masturbating in front of Caliph. Just when she thought he couldn't surprise—or arouse—her any more, he'd lay down his next challenge and she'd struggle to catch her breath, to summon her nerve.

He was a contradiction from the word go. She'd noticed that in the shop. Tonight, he'd fluctuated from tender lover to demanding Dom, constantly keeping her on her toes, struggling to keep up.

She'd come here with only a cursory knowledge of what it meant to be submissive to a man. While the concept never failed to inflame her whenever she read an erotic novel, there was a huge difference between fantasy and reality. She truly longed to play the submissive role, but she'd spent a lifetime trying to prove herself as a strong woman—even within her marriage—so she was struggling to make her head and her body agree.

Caliph didn't move as he waited for her to obey. She wasn't sure why touching herself as he watched felt harder than all the rest. He'd pushed some difficult limits tonight, but this one was the toughest. Which seemed ridiculous.

She started to move her hand toward her pussy, her eyes closing automatically. Maybe if she tried to forget he was there...

The mattress shifted and she opened her eyelids to find Caliph leaning over her. He lifted her head to place a pillow beneath it.

"Keep your eyes open and on my face. Don't look away."

Her jaw tensed. Damn man stripped all her defenses away. She scowled, but remained silent. He'd taken away her right to speak, but he'd also revealed his ability to read her expressions. She'd use that to her advantage.

His eyes narrowed. "Are you sure you want to test me, Jen?"

The question was laced with just enough sensual threat to send even more juices to her pussy. Maybe he should have left the drop cloth on the bed. If he kept playing with her like this, she'd drown them both in her arousal.

She smoothed out her features, aiming for a repentant look. She wasn't sure she'd pulled it off, but her contrition must have been enough because Caliph moved away, standing at the edge of the bed once more. His cock was hard as a rock, looking almost painful. He hadn't bothered to remove the condom. How could he deny himself something he so obviously needed?

"Time to stop stalling. Touch yourself. I want to see how you make yourself come."

She frowned again, but this time her response wasn't based on annoyance. She was worried. The truth was she'd never brought herself to climax with just her hands. Jennifer was the proud owner of an array of toys—sex aides she needed to provoke the response he was demanding now.

He crossed his arms, letting his impatience show.

Jennifer forced her gaze to remain on his face as she lightly stroked her clit. The touch was more powerful than she'd expected and she jerked slightly, shocked by the impact.

"Shit," she muttered, quickly pressing her lips together and hoping he hadn't heard her slip-up.

Of course, he had.

Caliph reached beneath her, gripping her ass in his large hands. It was still sore from his previous punishment, but he didn't let that stop him. He squeezed, adding pressure until she winced.

"That's the last reminder you're going to get, Jen. No talking. Period. Next time you say something without permission, I'm getting out my belt."

She blinked rapidly. He wouldn't dare. Would he?

Yeah. Part of her was fairly certain that was exactly what he'd do. She pursed her lips tightly, not willing to push him further.

He released her ass, then gestured for her to continue. She ran her fingers over her clit again, building up the speed and pressure quickly. While she'd come earlier, that orgasm was a distant memory now. It certainly hadn't done much to douse the desires still coursing through her veins.

Unfortunately, too many things were working against her. She couldn't relax with Caliph watching. She couldn't stop thinking—about every stupid freaking thing. Was this turning him on? Did her stomach look fat in this position? How bad did her hair look? Every insecurity pushed its way to the forefront until she became numb to her actions.

God, how long would he make her try before he realized she simply couldn't come this way? Her fingers weren't enough to push her over the edge, especially not with an audience.

After a few moments, Caliph's hand landed on hers, halting her motions.

Finally.

She started to lower her legs, but he shook his head.

"You ready to take this seriously?"

She frowned. "What do you—" She paused. Did that

count as a question he wanted answered?

He lifted one eyebrow and waited for her to respond. "Well?"

"What do you mean?"

"What were you thinking about just now, Jen?"

She blushed, unwilling to tell him for fear he'd realized how close to unhinged she really was.

"Were you thinking about me? About giving me what I'd asked for? Something I wanted?"

She licked her lips. Shit. She hadn't been thinking about him at all. Not really. She'd been more concerned with her own hang-ups. Her own reasons why she couldn't do what he'd requested.

She shook her head. "No."

His fingers tightened. Her hand was still pressed to her clit but his strong grip prevented her from withdrawing it. "Why not?"

Caliph kept forcing her to expose herself. She'd expected tonight to just be about sex, a brief foray into BDSM. She hadn't anticipated sharing more than her body. That much she'd been ready to give.

The rest?

Not so much.

"Caliph…" Her words dried up. "I'm sorry."

Her apology seemed to anger him and while she'd witnessed several of his stern looks, she'd never seen him truly angry. "Don't. Don't say that to me. I'm not your ex. I don't look at you and see flaws. Jesus. Stop worrying about stuff that doesn't matter and start concentrating on what's right."

As he spoke, he began to push her fingers against her clit once more. "This is right, Jen. What's going on between us is good. Hell, it's better than good, it's off-the-charts, fucking amazing."

He took control of her hand, molding it as if it was made of clay and he was sculpting a sex toy for her. He grasped two of her fingers, pressing them inside her pussy. She was overwhelmed by the heat, the moisture, the tight clenching and the sparks.

Oh my God.

It was electric.

Caliph determined the depth, the speed. "Add another finger."

She reacted without thought. Instead, she let him be her guide. His eyes never left hers and she let herself see—really see—what he felt. Something hard and cold melted inside her. The depression she'd allowed to fester and grow faded away.

He thought she was beautiful.

This is right, he'd said, and for the first time she let herself acknowledge that fact. Accept it.

He slowly released her hand, but she didn't hesitate, didn't give up the incredible rhythm he'd introduced. She thrust her fingers deeper as she added her thumb to the dance. Once, twice she drew it along her clit, fighting to keep her eyes open and on his. He wasn't hiding from her and she wanted to offer him the same. The pressure built, her hand moving on autopilot as she gave free reign to every astounding sensation.

Nothing mattered but this place, this moment. This man.

He wanted to see her come and it was a gift she was dying to give him.

She thrust one last time and flew away. Her back arched as she cried out loudly. She sensed Caliph moving, felt the bed dip. She was in the midst of her climax when his strong arms spread her legs farther apart. She screamed as he pushed his cock inside her, the powerful force, the beauty of being filled by him drove her to come again. Or was this still the original orgasm?

All she knew was she never wanted it to end.

Caliph didn't take her gently. His hard thrusts offered no reprieve, no time for rest or recovery.

She reached up, grasping his upper arms, needing to touch him. When that contact proved too little, she tried to pull him closer.

He dropped down to his elbows, his forearms lying next to her sides, his firm hands gripping her shoulders to hold her still.

Her ability to think deserted her as Jennifer gave herself over to the tactile, the emotions. She wanted to kiss him, so she did.

Caliph missed a beat when she clasped his face in her hands and pulled his lips to hers. Then he took over, his tongue mimicking the motions of his cock. He was claiming every part of her and she was glad to put the reins in his hands. The past year had been exhausting.

Now, tonight, Caliph was bearing the heavy load. It was the most wonderful thing anyone had ever done for her.

She wrapped her legs around his waist and tilted her hips higher, encouraging him to go deeper. He took the invitation.

Sweat slid along her brow as the temperature in the room increased.

Caliph released her lips, his breathing hot and heavy against her cheek. "Come with me, Jen."

She didn't have the strength to tell him she was already there. Her body stiffened as her orgasm crashed through her once more.

Caliph lowered his head to her shoulder, groaning. His motions slowed as he thrust inside her as deeply as he could go before holding there, his body jerking with his own climax.

Neither of them moved for several minutes. Caliph simply held himself above her as they slowly drifted back to earth.

Then, he pushed himself to her side, removing the condom and tossing it into a trashcan before tugging until her back was pressed against his chest, spoon-fashion.

His arm loosely wrapped around her, his hand covering one of her breasts in a way that was nothing less than familiar, possessive. Lovely.

She was the first to break the silence, not based on nerves—though she wasn't foolish enough to think they wouldn't return—but because she was riding a high. Giddy.

"You okay back there?"

He chuckled softly. "I think so. That was one hell of a ride, Jen."

She grinned, pleased by the gruff sound of his voice. It betrayed how exhausted he was. She liked the idea of wearing him out. That had certainly never happened before with any other man.

"It was incredible. I'm not sure I've ever experienced anything like that. I mean I've read lots of books about BDSM, but damn, there's a huge difference between imagining and doing. I didn't realize how intense it was going to be. I guess you're used to this sort of thing, but I have to admit…I didn't have a clue sex could be so, so…" She sighed. "I don't think anyone's invented a word to describe what I just felt."

Caliph placed a soft kiss on her shoulder. "Maybe we should think of one. Or we could just forget the vocabulary and do it all over again."

She laughed, twisting until she faced him. Despite his height and sheer muscle mass, their bodies fit. Perfectly. "Again? Really?" She ran her hand along his flaccid cock, surprised when it stirred and began to thicken. Caliph's stamina was off the charts. Her nipples budded in response.

Caliph noticed. He bent his head, sucking one of the tight buds into his mouth roughly. She groaned, silently hoping he'd repeat the action on the other nipple.

"Again," Caliph said. "Again and again."

Jennifer grinned, then she gasped.

Then she learned the true meaning of again.

All night long.

CHAPTER SIX

Caliph felt the heat of the sun on his bare skin, but didn't bother to open his eyes to acknowledge it was morning. He tightened his hold on Jennifer instead, enjoying the feeling of her hair tickling his chin, her hot breath caressing his chest. It wasn't uncommon for him to have sleepovers with lovers. Morning sex was one of his favorite things.

His lips tipped upward, the grin emerging as he recalled the previous night. Jennifer had been more than a pleasant surprise. She'd actually blown his misconceptions about her conservative nature out of the water. It seemed amazing to him that he'd considered—even for one second—that she was too innocent to accept his desires.

One night in and he began to wonder if he'd be able to keep up with her. He had thrown her into the deep end right out of the gate and while she'd struggled a bit to adapt, in the end, she'd taken to his demands, his darker desires, as if she'd been part of the lifestyle forever.

He'd invited her to stay for the weekend and he hoped she'd take him up on that offer.

Unfortunately, the morning-after glow he was experiencing clearly wasn't present for Jennifer.

"I think maybe I should head home," she said softly.

Caliph shook his head. "Nope."

He didn't bother to open his eyes. Even so, he could feel her smile against his chest. "Caliph—"

She intended to argue, but he wasn't in the mood to listen. He tilted her face up to his with his fingers. "I want the whole weekend, Jen. I'm not ready to let this go yet. There's still so much for us to explore. Besides, your car is parked at Midnight Ink, so you don't have any way to leave."

He placed a soft kiss on her forehead when she scowled at him.

"So basically I'm your prisoner?" Her tone told him exactly how much she didn't mind that.

"Yep. You're all mine for the rest of the day and tonight. Maybe tomorrow too. I'll have to see how my cock is holding up by then."

She laughed. "So does this kidnapping come complete with bondage? Because I fully intend to be a very naughty captive."

Jesus. He'd thought he'd woken up with a hard-on,

but her sexy taunt proved him wrong. His cock thickened even more. He rolled forward, climbing over Jennifer until she was caged beneath him. Grasping her wrists, he pulled her hands above her head, keeping a firm grip on them, letting her feel what it would mean to be helpless, at his mercy. "You sure you want me to tie you up?"

He'd paused several times last night, giving her a chance to adjust to his demands and to use her safe word if necessary. She'd never uttered it. Never given any indication she wanted to. Those kid gloves came off today.

Jennifer's breathing accelerated, her generous breasts rising and falling, almost distracting him from his question.

He pressed her hands against the pillow harder. "Answer me."

She nodded instantly. He'd noticed her responses came quicker the more demanding he became.

"Say it out loud."

"Yes." Her reply was a whisper, betraying exactly how much she wanted what he was offering. He didn't hesitate. Instead, he reached above her, searching for the straps already secured to the headboard. She gave him that same amused smile she'd offered last night when she discovered he had straps attached to his foot posts.

"Were you ever a Boy Scout?"

He got her joke instantly. "Nope, but that doesn't mean I don't know how to prepare for the really important events."

Her grin faded when he tied the first hand, tightening it until she couldn't move her arm at all. Last night, he'd left the bonds on her ankles relatively loose, introducing her to the sensation.

He didn't feel the need to do that again. Caliph wanted to push her further. Holding on to her free hand, he attached it as well until both wrists were bound directly above her head.

Caliph rose from the bed, walking to the foot of the mattress. Reaching forward, he grasped her ankles, tugging her entire body lower on the bed until her arms were stretched to the max. Then he hooked her ankles to the corner posts, leaving her legs open to him.

He admired his work as Jennifer flushed slightly. How many times would she blush before she became comfortable with his scrutiny?

She had definitely learned many of last night's lessons well. Rather than try to look away or hide from him, her gaze remained steadily on his while he studied her body. He'd decorated her skin with a different sort of art last night. Her lips were puffy and red from his kisses and there were several love bites around her neck and on her breasts. There were some small bruises on her thighs, left there when he'd held her open, fucking her roughly. He knelt between her outstretched legs and ran his fingers over them.

Jen lifted her head, watching. "They don't hurt."

He captured her gaze as he moved his hand higher.

Using the tip of one finger, he ran it along her slit, studying her face for a reaction. She was wet, ready for him. He was quickly becoming spoiled by her continual arousal. Nothing he did seemed to faze her, scare her. It was as if he'd molded his dream lover from clay and some magic had brought Jennifer to life and to his bed.

"Sore?"

As always, he was treated to her complete honesty. "A little. But I don't care."

He gave her a crooked grin. "I do."

She frowned. "You aren't going to stop, are you?"

He shook his head. "I probably should, but I can't. I'm too greedy when it comes to you."

She smiled. "Good. Now...will you please hurry up? I think I might be dying of horniness."

Caliph had never let any of his previous lovers—the submissive ones—speak to him so cheekily, but he loved her humor, her shy demands. This felt a lot less like a scene and more like a relationship.

As soon as the word crossed his mind, he realized the truth of it. He'd entered this bedroom with Jen, intent on exposing her wild side and introducing her to BDSM. And, of course, in return, he'd get to spend a sex-filled night with a hot woman.

Somewhere along the line, the desire to simply get laid had morphed into something more. Something better.

Unexpected.

And not entirely wanted.

While he wasn't opposed to long-term relationships, he'd always preferred an unencumbered life. One where he didn't have to answer to anyone.

"Caliph?"

Shit. He'd gone quiet too long. Time to snap out of it. Get this weekend back on course. He lifted his hand and slapped the inside of Jennifer's thigh.

She gasped.

"I need to explain the concept of topping from the bottom to you."

Jennifer bit her lip guiltily. "No, you don't. I've read about that in my dirty books. I know what it is."

Caliph slapped the other thigh, adding more bite, knowing exactly how to make it sting. "And yet you keep doing it."

"I can't help it." Her eyes darkened with lust. He'd noticed last night that her body responded as much to pain as to pleasure. Then she made him an offer he couldn't refuse. "Make me remember."

He took a deep breath, trying to keep calm as the Dom inside him emerged fully. God, she was a flirty little thing, every word she spoke provocative. Challenging.

"I'm going to gag you."

Jennifer exhaled sharply and started to speak.

"No. No talking, Jen. Hold up two fingers on your left hand."

She obeyed instantly.

"That's your safe word while the gag is in. If you want me to stop, hold up those two fingers. Understand?"

She nodded.

He walked to the corner of his bedroom, grabbing a bag. After Jennifer left Midnight Ink on Tuesday, he'd gone to the sex shop over his lunch break and picked up a few items. As the week passed, he'd returned to the store two more times as he fantasized even more ways he wanted to take her. He'd acquired quite a kinky collection and he was looking forward to using every single toy on her.

Last night, she'd distracted him from those plans, seducing him in ways he hadn't anticipated. Today, he intended to make up for lost time.

He pulled out the ball gag, then perused the other items in the bag. Fuck it. He picked up the entire package and returned to the bed with it. They'd use it all eventually.

Caliph bent over the side of the bed, lifting her head slightly to put the gag in her mouth, then securing it in place. She struggled against it initially and he glanced toward her hands. No signal.

"This morning's lesson is about obedience."

She blinked rapidly at the sound of his deep voice, then a line formed in her brow, warning him she would put up some resistance. With former lovers, he would have been annoyed by that look of defiance, expecting total submission from his bedmates. But with Jennifer, he looked forward to the challenge she represented.

He pushed the thought away. The damn woman was still getting under his skin and she couldn't even speak.

Grabbing the bag from the bed, he walked to the bathroom, opening all the packages, washing the array of toys he'd purchased. Jennifer wasn't going to know what hit her.

Returning to the room, he plucked the bullet vibrator from the pile and pushed it into Jennifer's pussy. No fanfare, no preparation—he already knew she was wet. He just pressed the toy in.

"You aren't allowed to come unless I give you permission."

Her eyes narrowed and he had no doubt she'd have disagreed if she could speak. He gave her a superior smile, then flipped the switch on the remote to high.

Jennifer jerked roughly, beautifully restrained by the straps on her wrists and ankles. She cried out, the sound muffled by the gag. He didn't lower the speed on the vibrator and made no move to touch her at all.

Instead he watched her struggle, trying to decide if she was fighting the orgasm or working to achieve it. With his rebellious lover, it could be either.

She hadn't fully embraced the concept of submission yet, though he knew the traits were there as well as her desire to accept them. It would take time for her to learn what it truly meant to give herself to him, to bend her will to his. She'd been on her own for nearly a year and she'd spent that time fighting to find her own strength, to make it through life without a man. It wasn't going to be easy for her to now release her grip on what she clearly viewed as progress and hand the control over to him.

He'd have to find a way to prove to her the power in this situation was hers.

He looked at her hands once more, searching for the sign. She may be fighting the sensations provoked by the vibrator, but she sure as hell didn't want to give up the war. Her hands remained firmly clenched into tight fists.

Jennifer's breathing increased and she moaned. The labored sound gave her away. Caliph turned off the remote.

Her expression reflected pure murder. Yep. She'd definitely been ready to come and, given her anger, it appeared she hadn't intended to hold back.

Caliph climbed onto the bed, hovering over her on his hands and knees. "Bad girl."

She shook her head, trying to dislodge the gag, but her hands remained closed.

"You've just sealed your fate, Jen. If you'd behaved, I

wouldn't have left you hanging for very long. Now the clock is set. You're not going to come for the next two hours."

She made a sound of protest.

"Keep it up and I'll make it three."

She huffed, but fell silent. Her eyes still promised retribution.

"You need to learn to school those expressions, Jennifer. Dirty looks are as bad as speaking without permission. Shoot any more of those daggers at me and I'll punish you."

Her reaction to the word *punish* went through him like an aphrodisiac. She wanted it. There was no denying that when her nipples budded and her eyes went soft.

"There are different types of punishment. Some you will enjoy, others you won't. Don't provoke my temper or you're going to learn that difference the hard way. That spanking last night had very little to do with correcting bad behavior. I did it primarily for your pleasure. If you continue to disobey me, I'm going to reprimand you in a way that brings you no satisfaction. Do you understand?"

She nodded slowly. Her arousal was beginning to wane, allowing uncertainty and confusion to creep in.

Caliph turned the vibrator on once more, only this time he set it on low.

Jennifer's eyes drifted closed, but her calmer response

told him this sensation wasn't enough for her. She tried to lift her hips toward him, but the straps held her almost completely immobile. She shuddered, clearly needing more stimulation.

He wasn't going to give it to her. Not yet. She was his for the next two hours and he intended to use that time to his advantage.

Bending his head, he sucked one of her nipples into his mouth. Jennifer groaned, arching her neck with delight. He'd been pleased to discover how sensitive her breasts were. Perhaps later, he'd bring her to orgasm simply with breast play, but for now, he had another plan.

Moving his head from one nipple to the other, he sucked and nipped at them until they were large, red, tight. Then he retrieved the clamps he'd bought. Jennifer's face told him instantly they were entering new territory. That knowledge excited him, fed his own arousal.

He placed a clamp on her left nipple as Jennifer's back bowed upward, sharp, harsh breaths escaping her nose as he tightened it. He used her breathing to let him know when the pain crossed from good to bad, then he dialed the screw back a notch.

Caliph repeated the process on her other nipple, then pushed up to kneel between her legs and admire his work. Thirty minutes had passed.

"I'm going to take the gag out, but you're still not allowed to speak."

Her face was calmer now, her expressive eyes silent for once. Caliph recognized the look. She'd stopped listening to her conscience, moving beyond the logical, embracing the visceral. He unhooked the gag and removed it. Gently he wiped her lips and lightly massaged her jaw.

Unable to resist, he bent down to kiss her. Kissing had never been a big part of any scene for him, but there was something about Jennifer that made him want to coddle her as much as he wanted to dominate. It was slightly unnerving, but—like her—he was finished thinking about this. From this moment on, he simply wanted to give in to his desires.

Jennifer returned his kiss, her tongue stroking his. When he pulled away, her face lifted, trying to keep him close. If her hands had been free, he had no doubt she would have latched onto his neck to hold his lips to hers.

She wanted him—really wanted him.

In the past, he'd indulged in casual affairs. No woman had ever acted as if he was vital to her. They'd just taken their own pleasures and moved on.

Before this weekend, Caliph would never have admitted to enjoying a woman who needed him so much, but Jennifer's subtle *stay with me* overtures touched him. Turned him on.

She narrowed her eyes when he picked up the remote to the vibrator once more. Then he watched her suck in a deep breath and hold it to prepare herself. He pushed it up a notch to medium, holding the high speed in reserve. Her body tensed in her effort to stave off her orgasm. Caliph was impressed by her willingness to satisfy him, to give him what he wanted.

"And now things get serious."

She frowned, but didn't reply. Didn't even attempt to.

Leaving the bed, he walked to her feet and untied the straps. He massaged her ankles for a few moments, then told her to bend her knees, leaving her legs open.

She obeyed. Caliph wondered if she'd accept the next position as easily. He removed the straps from the bottom of the bed and attached them to eyehooks higher on the opposite sides of his headboard.

She watched his movements in silence, but he could read the concern—and doubt—on her face.

Once the bindings were in place, he knelt on the bed and lifted her legs, keeping a firm grip on her ankles. He tugged them upward until she was bent in half. Then he bound them with her legs straight above her head.

"Does that hurt?"

She shook her head.

"Good." He ran his hand over her bare ass, enjoying exactly how much this position left her vulnerable. Open.

He cupped her breasts and gave a firm squeeze to the fleshy mounds. It increased the pressure to the clamps.

Jennifer's eyes closed and she groaned blissfully. The sound must have shocked her, causing her to panic. She looked at him to gauge his reaction.

Caliph chuckled. "I said you can't speak. Those cute little sex sounds are definitely allowed. In fact…"

He ran his fingers along her slit, enjoying her soft whimper. A glance at the clock confirmed an hour had passed. His cock was rock-hard and reading him the riot act for holding off. Caliph wrapped his fist around his erection and slowly stroked the sensitive flesh as Jennifer watched.

She licked her lips and, for a moment, he was tempted to move over her and push his cock into her wet, hot mouth. He resisted the urge. This scene was meant to push her limits, test her ability to obey his demands no matter what. There was still work to do.

Reaching back into the bag of toys, he retrieved a tube of lubrication and a butt plug. She'd confessed last night she'd never indulged in anal play, but her tone when she mentioned it told him her curiosity outweighed her fears. That seemed to be true for most of her desires. Jennifer had yet to balk at a single thing he'd suggested or tried.

Taking the cap off the tube, he squeezed some onto his finger, then rubbed it around her anus. She wiggled slightly, but didn't try to move away. She also didn't say her safe word. Caliph realized he'd stopped listening for it. The previous night, the word was never far from his mind as he'd expected it to pop out at any time. Today, they'd turned a corner. He'd learned to read her responses, to know what she genuinely liked.

He added more lube to his finger, pressing it inside her ass. Jennifer's breathing had regulated, but with this new sensation, it sped up, became louder. He worked the lubricant into her ass, adding more and more. Then one finger became two and two became three. He initiated her to the act slowly, giving her tight, virgin muscles time to adjust to the unfamiliar invasion.

Jennifer's moans became louder as he finger-fucked her ass, adding speed and strength to each thrust. His balls drew tight. What would he give to pull his hand away and fuck her there with his cock?

Someday. Soon.

Then he wondered if she'd give him another night, another weekend. His initial desire for a one-night stand had been rejected as true greediness took over. He wanted more. A lot more.

Her panting breaths alerted him to how close she was to coming. He withdrew. Time wasn't up. She growled, the sound reflecting anger more than arousal. He lifted his hand and swatted her ass in warning. Jennifer lifted her bottom as much as the straps would allow, silently begging for more. He indulged her request, mainly because there was nothing he loved more than spanking her ass, watching it turn red under his hand. He placed several more blows to her bottom as Jennifer's back arched and her cries grew louder.

Christ. She was in danger of coming merely from a spanking. Once again, Caliph stopped. She shuddered roughly as she attempted to fight back her desire to come.

The game was far from over. Lifting the butt plug, he coated it with lubrication, then slowly pressed it into her ass. Jennifer's eyes drifted closed as she whispered his name. He didn't chastise her for speaking without permission. She was drifting into subspace—he could read it in her face, in her responses.

He wondered if his next action would drag her back or push her further into her state of bliss. He hoped the latter.

Once the plug was in place, he leaned forward and reached for a clamp. He briefly considered warning her about the pain to come, but didn't want to ruin the moment with words. She was floating and if his suspicions about her need for pain proved true, this would only add to the experience.

He removed the clamp.

Jennifer jerked. "Oh my God."

Caliph had anticipated the response, her shock when she felt that initial jolt of pain. He was there, waiting for her. He put his lips over her sore nipple, caressing it with soft strokes of his tongue and gentle sucks until she calmed down.

She stiffened in preparation when he moved to tug the second clamp free. He repeated the same ministrations, helping to turn the pain into something more pleasurable. He took his time, acknowledging how easy it would be to spend hours playing with her breasts. They were full and sensitive.

Then he felt her stir. He lifted his head and found her eyes on his. He knew what she wanted, but the selfish man inside wanted to hear it from her lips.

"Say it," he prompted.

"Please," she whispered. "I need you."

Heaven to his ears. He didn't bother to look at the clock. It was close enough. Reaching above her head, he released her ankles, then her hands. He removed the bullet, tossing it aside.

"Wrap your legs around my waist and hold on, love."

She followed his command, gasping when he placed his cock at her opening. The plug was still in her ass, but he didn't plan to remove it. It would only heighten the pleasure. Then he paused.

"Shit. Condom."

He started to reach for the nightstand, but she halted him. "Do you have to use one?"

He frowned. "I'm clean, Jen, but—"

"So am I. And I'm on birth control."

He blew out a long, hard breath. He'd never taken a woman without a condom. Not once. In his entire life.

Neither one of his previous long-term girlfriends had been able to take the Pill without getting sick, so he had been in charge of taking the necessary precautions.

"You're sure?" he asked.

She nodded. "Come inside me."

There was a double meaning to her request. And both offers were too good to pass up.

Caliph pushed in slowly, his chest constricting as he forgot how to breathe. He wasn't sure he'd ever felt anything so powerful, so freaking amazing.

As much as he tried to savor the moment, to prolong the beauty of it, his measured pace didn't help. Jennifer had been riding the razor's edge too long. She shook beneath him and he realized she was still trying to hold off. He pressed in to the hilt, leaned down and kissed her lightly on the cheek. "Come for me, Jen."

He started to move, just a slight withdrawal before pushing deeper. It was all she needed. Her body stiffened as she released a loud, keening cry. Her inner muscles clamped down on his aching cock and she dragged her fingernails down his bare back—leaving some serious artwork of her own on his skin.

Caliph closed his eyes and fought to regulate his breathing. He didn't want this to end too soon. He rode out the storm of her powerful orgasm, then—when calmness began to descend once more—he thrust harder, choosing his favorite rhythm, speed.

Jennifer wrapped her legs tighter around him, spurring him on, accepting his rough claiming. When her pussy clenched again, he realized she was on the verge of yet another orgasm. He'd never be able to resist coming this time.

Jennifer trembled with the second orgasm and Caliph joined her, giving in to his own pleasure. The impact of his climax would have knocked him down had he been standing. Jet after jet of come exploded from him, each pulse sending electricity up and down his spine.

What a weekend.

As soon as he was able to move—his strength had deserted him—he fell to her side, pleased when Jennifer rolled, curling against his chest, soft and warm as a newborn kitten. She was asleep within seconds. He wouldn't be far behind. Caliph tucked her closer with an arm around her shoulders, enjoying the feel of her next to him. For the first time, it felt like someone belonged here. With him. In his bed.

Jennifer fit.

He'd told her she was a blank canvas, that her future was hers to design, to color. But now he wondered if he hadn't been a bit blank himself. The colorful life he thought he'd been living suddenly felt bland, a whole lot of off-white and gray. In a few short days, Jennifer had added shocking reds, cool blues and vivid purples, opening his eyes to opportunities he'd never considered.

His eyes drifted closed, a heavy warmth coursing

through him.

Then he contemplated what happened when the weekend came to a close and the contentment started to wane as reality crashed around him.

The next move wasn't his to make.

It was hers.

CHAPTER SEVEN

Jennifer tightened her grip around Caliph's waist as the motorcycle sped up. She'd spotted the Harley in Caliph's driveway as they had walked toward his car and admitted she'd never ridden on one. He had taken her admission as something akin to a mortal sin, thrown a helmet on her head and now they were headed to Midnight Ink to retrieve her car.

Sunday had arrived and the weekend was officially over.

They had spent most of the day—and two nights—before in his bed and had only woken up a couple hours earlier, after which they'd showered together. She had joked that they both looked as if they'd been ridden hard and put away wet, after she complained about her stiff muscles and he winced when he tried to put a shirt on over the deep scratches she'd left on his back.

Breakfast had been a quiet affair, both of them

talking about a whole bunch of nothing. Truth was Jennifer hadn't known what to say, so she'd filled the silence with nonsense about the weather and past Mardi Gras parties.

She'd been both relieved and disappointed when they'd hopped on the motorcycle because it didn't give them an opportunity to talk on the way to the shop.

Caliph took the long way to Midnight Ink, treating her to a quick ride on Pontchartrain Expressway so he could rev up the motor and gain some serious speed. She clung tighter to his waist, enjoying the roar of the engine, the vibrations, the sense of flying. Just when she thought Caliph couldn't make this weekend any more amazing, he found a way to take her breath away once more. She'd been in a constant state of exhilaration and it was addictive.

As he pulled up to the tattoo shop, her heart began to race. The idea of not seeing him again was extremely unappealing. For a split second, she even considered signing on for another tattoo just to prolong their association, but she quickly dismissed that idea with a soft laugh.

Caliph dismounted the bike, then helped her off. She handed him the helmet.

"What did you think of the ride?"

She knew he was asking about the spin on the motorcycle, but her sex-soaked mind went straight back to the bedroom. "It was incredible." There…that covered it all.

Caliph was obviously pleased by her response. "I'm glad you enjoyed it. I was afraid I'd scare you."

"Never." She'd never spoken a truer word. Then her mouth went dry. This was it. "Well…"

Jennifer's brain failed as she sought for something to say. Some way to tell him what this weekend had meant to her. And to ask for more.

She'd never do that. It wasn't in her chemical makeup to be so assertive. At work, she could make her wishes known clearly and without hesitance, but when it came to grasping anything for herself, she floundered like a fish out of water. Hell, when Marcus told her he was having an affair and asked for the divorce, she'd merely nodded. It wasn't until he'd packed up all his stuff and left the house that she found the raging words she wished she'd said.

And as far as this affair with Caliph was concerned, she knew what she wanted, but she didn't feel confident enough to say it aloud only to have him reject her. She'd ridden the rejection train before and, quite frankly, it sucked.

Unfortunately, Caliph had taken her on adventures her sex-starved, fairly vivid imagination hadn't even thought to conjure up. He hadn't just ruined her for other men. He'd made sure she wouldn't be able to escape into her books anymore without wishing she were the heroine and he the hero in every story. So much for fictional therapy.

"I had a really great time." The inane words were nearly accompanied by a wince, but she managed to school her features just in time.

Caliph nodded slowly. "So did I. You're an incredible woman, Jen."

She wasn't feeling very incredible right now. In fact, all she felt was pure terror. So she instituted the standard quick escape. "Well, I guess I'll see you around."

She backed up her lame farewell with the most ridiculous platonic hug in history. God, she gave her distant cousin, the one she only saw every third year at the family reunions, a more familiar embrace.

Caliph was frowning when she stepped away, but she couldn't summon enough courage to do more than lift her hand in a lighthearted wave before she turned and all but sprinted to her car.

By the time she'd buckled herself into the driver's seat and found the nerve to turn around and look back toward the shop, Caliph had entered the building.

She fell forward as she lightly pounded her forehead on the steering wheel.

"Stupid fucking girl," she muttered, completely disgusted with herself.

What the hell had she done?

The answer resounded in her head like a cathedral bell. She'd reverted to character. The Jennifer who'd arrived at Caliph's house on Friday night had returned with a vengeance, running like a scared mouse at the first sign of rejection.

God, she was an idiot.

She hated that woman. The one who'd sat quietly and let her husband of seventeen years break her heart and walk away without one word of anger. The one who'd wasted a year of her life mourning over a man who didn't deserve her.

The one who'd just let the coolest, hottest, kindest man she'd ever met go without telling him exactly how wonderful he was.

If she could manage the position, she felt the overwhelming desire to get out of the car and kick her own ass.

No. Screw this. This life. This eternal hell.

She wanted more and, by God, she was going for it.

Before she could think of any reason why it was a bad idea, she was out of her car and standing at the door to Midnight Ink. She pushed the door open with way more force than she should have, the bell above it making her jump as it jingled.

While her arrival seemed unnervingly showy to her, it didn't appear to have caught anyone's notice.

"Caliph," she said, louder than she'd intended. The only other person in the shop was a woman Jennifer hadn't seen before. She assumed this was Rosie, the female tattoo artist Caliph had mentioned.

Caliph glanced up. He'd been standing next to his chair, staring into his cup of coffee like a zombie.

"Jen?"

"I don't, I mean, I was hoping…" God, she sounded like a complete tool.

"Say it."

His tone was one of pure command, the sound reminding her of everything that had passed between them. It spoke to her on some level she'd never acknowledged or noticed prior to this weekend with him. And it left her so damn hot, she felt as if she could burst into flames.

"I want to see you again."

She could feel the other woman staring at her, but Jennifer pushed through her embarrassment, her nervousness. She'd spent two days and only a handful of hours prior to the weekend with Caliph, yet he'd done more to help her find her feet, her strength than months' worth of conversations with well-meaning friends after her divorce. "I'd really like to go out with you again."

She held his gaze and let her words stand, willing to take this risk. If he told her he wasn't interested, she would be hurt. But she wouldn't fall apart. She wasn't the fragile woman Marcus had left nearly a year ago. She'd proven she could pick up the pieces and move on. There was a big difference between needing a man in your life and wanting one.

And she wanted this one...for as long as it lasted. If that wasn't forever, then so be it. There were plenty of other fish in the sea, petals on her daisy. One day, she'd find the one who would love her for who she was, who would make her happy. And even if she didn't, she intended to live a life without regrets.

Caliph grinned. "I'd like to keep seeing you too."

"You would?" Damn insecure Jennifer crept out at the most annoying times.

Caliph didn't seem to mind. He laughed. "Yeah. I would. In fact, I'd like to nail down our next date right now. Make this decision official before you try to run away again. You realize that was the worst morning-after goodbye in history, right?"

She laughed, relief flowing through her like a hot shower on a cold winter's night. "Yeah. My brain wasn't fully functioning back there. Luckily it caught up to my stupid mouth before I drove away."

He walked over to her. "So what about that date?"

"I'm free next weekend."

He shook his head. "Too far away. Dinner. Tomorrow night."

Jennifer didn't even need to consider her schedule. She'd make it work. "Deal. I'll cook for you at my place to make up for being such a jackass."

Caliph grasped her hand and pulled her closer. "Food is a good way to apologize, but I can think of a better one."

"Dirty bastard."

He wrapped his arm around her and pinched her ass as she giggled. "Don't remember hearing any complaints when I had you tied to my bed yesterday."

Jennifer had forgotten they weren't alone until she heard the woman at the next station laugh.

"TMI," the other woman joked.

Caliph chuckled, then did the introductions. "Jen, this is Rosie. Rosie, this is Jennifer."

Like Sassy, Rosie was sporting some fun colored streaks in her hair, not to mention some serious ink on her arms and collarbone. For a moment, Jennifer considered asking Rosie where she got her hair done. She wouldn't mind adding a bit of color—maybe purple—to her own long tresses.

Rosie gave her a quick up-and-down glance. "So this is the daisy tattoo girl."

Jennifer looked at Caliph curiously.

Rosie answered her unspoken question. "He was a maniac last week, waiting—not very patiently—to see you again on Friday. Glad to see you two had a good time."

"We did."

Rosie studied Caliph's face. "And I'm glad to hear you're willing to see him again tomorrow. Something tells me he's not going to get you out of his system for quite a while."

Jennifer laughed, flattered to hear he had been looking forward to their date as much as her. "I hope not."

Her quick response appeared to have won Rosie's approval. The pretty tattoo artist looked at Caliph. "Well done, my friend."

The bell jangled over the door as a handsome, hulking blond man entered.

"Hello, sweetheart."

Rosie's face lit up as she walked away from them without a second glance.

Caliph leaned closer to whisper in her ear. "That's Finn. I haven't been the only maniac around here lately. Finn seems to make the rest of us mortals disappear in Rosie's world."

Jennifer understood the feeling. Whenever she was with Caliph, it felt as if they were the only two people on the planet.

"You in a hurry?" Caliph asked her.

She shook her head. One of the best parts of her job was that she—as senior hotel manager—got the weekends off.

"Good. Come here."

Caliph grasped her hand and tugged her through a door that led to a storage area in the back. He threw the lock on the door.

"What are you—"

Her question was cut off when Caliph grabbed her, kissing her so passionately her head spun. The embrace could have lasted for minutes or months for all Jennifer knew.

When he finally released her, he looked at her with stern, serious eyes. "I should punish you for that stunt you pulled in the parking lot. I thought you were really leaving."

"I thought I was too."

"What stopped you?"

"I'm tired of being a doormat." The words flew out without thought and she realized they weren't entirely correct. "I can't keep standing on the sidelines of my own life like some uninterested observer. I felt more alive this past weekend than I have in years. God, maybe even decades. It was a good feeling."

The laugh lines beside his eyes became more pronounced as she spoke. His smile grew wider.

"We're complete opposites, Caliph, and maybe this

fling is just going to be that. A fling. But for now, it's exactly what I need."

Caliph tilted his head and studied her face. "I'm cool with riding this out, seeing where it takes us. The weekend wasn't enough for me, Jen. I want more of you."

Her stomach fluttered at his admission—with anticipation and desire. "I can't imagine there's much of me left to claim. You explored a hell of a lot of uncharted territory this weekend."

He laughed. "Oh, trust me, love. We haven't even touched the tip of the iceberg."

She made a face, pretending to be worried, which made him laugh louder.

"In fact," he said as he reached out and grasped her waist, pulling her hips against his, "I think we should seal this dating deal with a kiss."

"Just a kiss?" she asked when his lips were a mere breath away from hers.

"We'll start with that. Then see where it leads." He ran his hands over her ass, squeezing them firmly. "After all, there's nothing I love more than covering this pretty canvas of yours with color."

She rubbed her cheek against his, savoring the sensation of her soft to his rough. "Pervert," she whispered.

Caliph laughed. "Definitely. But you're kinky, so that

makes us even."

Jennifer turned at the same time as Caliph, their lips finding each other's, though neither of them sought to turn the touch into a kiss. "Caliph?"

"Hmm?"

"Have you ever had sex back here?"

He chuckled. "Nope."

"Wanna do something really wicked?"

He laughed, then tugged on her hair with just enough force to get her engine revving. "I might have a few things we could try, kinky girl. Take off your clothes."

CRASH POINT

CHAPTER ONE

"I know, Mama. Yeah…Yeah…Mmmhmm."

Blake Mills leaned against the doorframe of the studio. He watched the petite blonde—who had her back turned to him—set up her camera equipment while balancing her cell phone between her shoulder and cheek. Her head was fully tilted to the right, yet she worked with ease.

"I understand how important this fundraiser is, Mama. I'm just not all that jazzed about taking a bunch of beefcake pictures of some brainless mimbos with more muscles than sense."

Blake stifled the urge to clear his throat, slightly offended by the photographer's insult, but he let it slide, unwilling to let her know he was there. He'd never been referred to as a male bimbo before. Even so, he was fairly certain he'd find a way to make her eat those words. He might not be the smartest guy on the planet, but he wasn't an airhead with a penis either.

The woman sighed heavily, continuing to speak. It occurred to him there was something vaguely familiar about her voice.

For now, he held his tongue, intent on enjoying the

view as she bent over to retrieve something from her camera bag, her firm, perfect ass pointed in his direction. She wore skintight jeans that accentuated the bottom half of her generous hourglass just right.

"Fine," she said in reply to something her mother had said. "I won't insult the models. At least not to their faces. But I'm reserving the right to make fun of them at Sunday dinner. I can't believe that last guy was able to squeeze his ego through the front door."

Ah, Blake thought, her annoyance started to make sense. The last guy had been a tool. He sympathized with the pretty woman. He'd been roped into this charity calendar bullshit too. Sounded like neither he, nor the photographer, were here willingly.

She stood up with her back still to him as she snapped her camera onto the tripod. It was clear her mother was giving her an earful by the short, cutoff replies the photographer was making.

"Yeah, but…"

"I know that. All I'm…"

"Alright, I can…"

Finally the woman pulled her cell away from her ear and mimicked the action of throttling it. Blake lost his ability to remain silent. He chuckled.

The photographer turned to face him and he sucked in an astonished breath.

Fuck.

Chloe Lewis.

For the briefest of moments, he hoped she wouldn't recognize him. After all, ten years had passed.

That wish was squashed instantly.

Her eyes narrowed when she saw him. "I have to go, Mama." She didn't even wait for her mother to say goodbye. Instead, she clicked the end button and slid the cell into her back jeans pocket. It was on the tip of his tongue to express surprise that she could squeeze anything else into the tight denim, but he was starting this conversation on thin ice as it was. No need to make it worse. Though there had always been something about Chloe that had him longing to tease her…just so he could hear her loud, joyful laughter. He'd never met anyone before or since who could laugh with such unrestrained, utter delight.

It was the first thing that had drawn him to her all those years ago. Chloe had trapped him in her tractor beam within minutes of their initial introduction and held him there for months—the best summer of his life. There was no denying the two of them had set off fireworks together—in and out of the bedroom. He'd never understood the word *tumultuous* until that summer. Perhaps enough time had passed that Chloe would forgive him and they could let bygones be bygones.

Chloe's eyes flashed fire.

Nope. No bygones.

"Hey, Chloe. Good to see you."

It was clearly the wrong opening. "Fuck you, Blake."

He deserved that. Even so, his pride—the same pride that had screwed things up between them so many years ago—surfaced. "I'm game if you are."

"That's it. Last straw. I'm not doing this. My mother can find someone else to take these damn pictures." She turned away from him, reaching for her phone, intent on calling her mother back.

He walked across the room and wrapped his hand around her wrist to stop her. "Wait."

She whirled on him, her temper blowing fast and hot. It took all the strength in his body not to grin. A smile when she was in the midst of an explosion was tantamount to committing suicide. Chloe may be small, but her boxer of a father and three older brothers had taught her well when it came to self-defense. Hell, it might be more accurate to say they'd given her brilliant lessons in all-out offensive attacks.

"Don't touch me."

Blake didn't remove his hand. Maybe the term *mimbo* did work for him. He'd never been accused of being too bright. Trying to keep hold of this miniature raging bull proved that. "Don't quit because of me."

She struggled to escape, but he merely tightened his

grip. His body had shifted into overdrive the second he'd gotten close enough to smell her floral perfume and feel the undeniable heat that rose up every time the two of them got within a few feet of each other.

He could tell Chloe felt it as well. Her chest rose and fell rapidly and her face was flushed. Their brief scuffle hadn't produced either side effect. It was the same for him. Two minutes with her and he was on fire, his cock hard enough to pound nails in concrete.

When it became obvious he wasn't going to release her, she froze, her body rigid with fury…and arousal. Even after all these years, he knew her well enough to recognize both.

"The committee is going to have to find another photographer. I've hit my limit on manhandling for the day."

It was the only thing she could have said that would have prompted him to loosen his grip. He dropped her hand. "What do you mean manhandling?"

She closed her eyes as if praying for patience. Blake had provoked that response in her no less than a million times in the past. And as always, it hit him like the world's most powerful aphrodisiac. He still drove her crazy. For some reason, that idea turned him on even more.

"How the hell did you get involved in this calendar, Blake? I can't imagine the committee actually thought it was a good idea to include some punk-ass biker as part of the collection." Then her gaze sharpened. "Did my mom call you to do this?"

He shook his head quickly. "Of course not." He hadn't seen Mama Lewis in nearly a decade. The same day he'd hopped on his motorcycle and driven away from Chloe without a word. He'd been a fool. Chloe had been adorable, cute at nineteen. At twenty-nine, she was a fucking knockout.

"I doubt your mom even knows I'm involved. I drew the short straw this morning down at the precinct. My captain's wife is on the committee and decided the NOPD needed to be represented. Captain Rogers isn't exactly known for being organized. He forgot to round someone up until today when his wife showed up and read him the riot act for it. Next thing I know, I'm on my way here."

Chloe's brows furrowed in confusion. "NOPD? Precinct?" Then she erupted in laughter…and it was just as Blake had remembered. Loud. Infectious. "Dear God, please tell me they didn't let you join the police force."

He smiled. "Detective Mills, at your service. Just got promoted to the Special Victims Unit last fall."

She shook her head, her mirth dying as she realized he was telling her the truth. Chloe was allowed her shock. There was a big part of him that still couldn't believe he'd joined the force. For most of his life, he'd half-expected his future to include time spent behind bars, not escorting others there.

"You're joking."

"Nope. Wanna see my handcuffs?" He winked at her wickedly, letting her know exactly how he'd use them on her.

She scowled. "It's not possible. There's no way—"

"I'm a cop, Chloe." He whipped out his badge and flashed it at her.

She reached into her back pocket to retrieve her cell phone. "It doesn't matter. I'm still calling my mother. Surely there has to be someone who can—"

"Take pictures as good as you? Not likely, CJ Lewis."

Shock registered on her face when he used her pen name. Chloe had made a name for herself in the world of photography, having published a collection of her work called *The Face of New Orleans*. Blake had spotted it in the window of a bookstore and bought it instantly. He couldn't begin to count the hours he'd poured over the pictures, amazed by her talent and her eye for hidden beauty. She'd captured the people of New Orleans perfectly, bringing their hometown to life in vivid color.

"How did you know that was me?"

He ran his finger along her cheek, trying not to let her see how much it hurt him when she winced and pulled away. What was he expecting? He'd broken her heart. "I always knew you'd find success with your photographs, Chloe Jeannette. You were too talented not to." He also knew she'd been named after both her grandmothers.

"You remembered my middle name?"

He nodded. It was strange how much he recalled about Chloe. There were times when Blake thought he recalled her life story better than his own. At nineteen, he'd hung on her every word, certain she was the most beautiful, fascinating girl he'd ever met. Now, he was finding the woman she'd become just as enthralling.

"Chloe, this is an important project and you know it. The money raised is going to a good cause. Besides, do you really want to call Mama Lewis and tell her you're bailing? You think that would be a fun phone call?"

Chloe shuddered. "She doesn't know *you're* here, that you're involved. I might actually get a bye based on that."

His grin grew, causing her frown to deepen. "Your mom always liked me."

"Liked. As in past tense. Then you stole her favorite wedding gift, cleaned out her wallet and made me cry. I suspect she'd be in the front of the line, even before my brothers, to kick your ass."

Blake was sure she was right. And that thought hurt. He'd always adored Chloe's mother. She was the only mom in history who hadn't taken one look at his ripped-up jeans, leather jacket and bad attitude, then issued an order for him to get the hell away from her daughter. Instead, she'd invited him in for Sunday dinner, engaged him in conversation and seen something of value inside him that Blake couldn't see himself at the time.

Then he'd betrayed Mama Lewis' belief that he'd do the right thing, rejected Chloe and run off like a thief in the night.

No. Not *like*. Literally a thief. He'd stolen two hundred dollars from Mama Lewis' purse and a silver serving platter.

"I'm sorry, Chloe."

She studied his face for several quiet moments. He didn't bother to hide. He wanted her to see, to read the sincerity in his words. His life was overflowing with regrets, but stealing from Chloe's family and leaving her ranked at the very top of the list.

"Maybe you are. But you're not forgiven." Her words were hard, final.

And not at all surprising. Because he'd stolen more from Chloe than just some money. He'd taken her virginity and her young girl's love and trust and he'd trampled all over it.

"I'll tell my captain to find someone else from the NOPD to pose for the calendar. You're more valuable to the project than I am."

She nodded. "Fine."

He took one last look at her, wondering how long—if ever—it would be until their paths crossed again. Would he have to wait months? Years? Longer? He'd thought of her more than he cared to admit over the past decade—her face often the last one he saw when he closed his eyes at night. He'd always wondered if she was happy, if she'd married or fallen in love, had kids. A quick glance at her bare ring finger answered the marriage question.

The idea of never seeing her again was more painful than he would have imagined. "Goodbye, Chloe."

He turned to leave, but his exit was cut short when Captain Rogers' wife appeared with two other women in tow. "Oh, Detective Mills, I'm so glad we caught you and Chloe before you started. My friends and I were just heading out for lunch and I wanted them to meet you." She turned to the women with her, briefly introducing them as fellow committee members. "I was absolutely delighted when you volunteered for this project."

"Short straw, huh?" Chloe muttered.

"I was afraid my husband was going to have to recruit someone unwilling. Heaven only knows how that would have turned out." Mrs. Rogers turned to Chloe, beaming. "Didn't I send you a wonderful subject? And I have no doubt his bio for the calendar will be the most impressive one. After all, he received the Medal of Valor when he saved two people from a burning building and his work with juveniles has been truly inspiring. Speaking of bios," Mrs. Rogers pulled several sheets of paper from her purse. "Here's Blake's bio, along with two others. I told your mother I'd drop them off to you today."

Blake didn't turn to look at Chloe. He hated being the center of attention. He'd done his job, nothing more. To hear Mrs. Rogers going on and on about his accomplishments like he was some sort of freaking superhero made him uncomfortable.

"I didn't do anything more than any other officer on the force would have done." He hoped that answer would be enough to kill the subject. It wasn't.

Mrs. Rogers was on a roll. "Plus he was instrumental in shutting down a major drug ring. My husband said it was the first time in all his years he felt a spark of hope for our local kids. Blake ensured there would be a lot fewer dealers on the playgrounds. All of this and he's only been on the force for five years."

Taking down that drug ring was one of the hardest things he'd ever done in his life—because it had involved him arresting his own father. That was one of the lowest moments in Blake's life, and to hear Mrs. Rogers discussing it as an accolade made him sick to his stomach.

"Actually, Mrs. Rogers, I'm afraid I'm not going to be able to—"

"Take the pictures today," Chloe interjected. "Detective Mills and I were just discussing some possible locales."

Blake turned to look at Chloe. She'd just threatened to walk off the project if he was involved. Now it sounded as if she was volunteering to make the job even harder. Locales?

Mrs. Rogers frowned, confused. "I was under the impression all the photographs would be shot here in your studio."

"That was the original plan, but after talking to the

detective, it occurred to me that the photos would be more interesting if they were taken in a variety of locations and included something that reflected each man's interests."

Blake nodded, not about to miss this opportunity to spend more time with Chloe. "I'm into motorcycles, so we were thinking of riding out to Lake Pontchartrain and snapping some shots. Or we even discussed the possibility of taking River Road and posing at the plantations."

Chloe scowled, but didn't contradict him. The two of them had spent hours flying up and down the highways on his bike when they were younger. The plantations on River Road and the lake had been their favorite destinations. Blake had only gotten his motorcycle—an ancient Harley he'd seen an ad for in the classifieds—that summer. Chloe had been shocked to discover he'd never seen anything outside of the city limits, so she'd made it her mission to expose him to all the beautiful places he'd missed. In a few months, she'd done a great job of opening his eyes to the world just outside the city.

Mrs. Rogers clapped her hands together. "Oh! This sounds wonderful. Even better than we'd hoped. Well then, don't let us distract you from your work. I can't wait to see the end result."

With that, Mrs. Rogers and her friends left in a flurry of excited chatter.

Blake crossed his arms. "I thought you wanted me out."

"I did, but how could I explain wanting to kick out

such an icon of the police force?"

"I was going to take the fall. Tell them I wasn't comfortable taking my shirt off for the picture."

Chloe snorted. "Yeah. I'm sure they would have believed that."

He grinned. "Are you saying I'm immodest?"

"I spent an entire summer with you and I can recall you wearing a shirt less than a handful of times. Usually at my mother's Sunday dinners and only then because she said you had to."

Blake rolled his eyes at her exaggeration, though when he considered it, she had a good point. That summer had been hot as hell and they'd spent most of it on his motorcycle, traveling an hour to the Gulf Coast beaches. Or riding beside the Mississippi. Or walking along the French Quarter. Or wrapped up in each other's arms. "I can come up with another reason to bail."

She shook her head. "No. I'm a professional and it's no big deal. I'll snap a few pictures, then you and I can go our separate ways again."

"In other words, you're afraid of your mother and Mrs. Rogers."

She shot him a dirty look, then said, "Yeah. I've decided you're the lesser of two evils."

He chuckled, then stepped closer, enjoying the way she held his gaze as he leaned down. "I fully intend to change your mind about that."

Blake had to give Chloe credit. The woman never backed down from any challenge. "I'm not worried."

Before he could think better of it, Blake closed the distance between them, placing a quick, hard kiss on her lips.

It was just as he'd remembered—only better. Chloe's lips were soft and she tasted so damn sweet—like peppermint and chocolate and sunshine all rolled up into one.

He'd spent most of his younger life around jaded, hard women who smelled of booze and cigarettes. However, since joining the police force, his dating life had dwindled down to nothing. Blake had been more celibate than a monk the past year or so. He hadn't minded that state until he'd seen her again.

He broke the union before Chloe had a chance to reject him…or knee him in the balls.

He tapped her nose playfully. "You should be. I'll call you later about the photo shoot."

Blake made his escape quickly before Chloe changed her mind about his participation in the project. He'd been ready to accept her dismissal and walk away. Until that kiss.

Now…well, now…he was driving without brakes. And the crash was imminent.

He grinned as he walked back out into the sunshine, grabbing his helmet and pulling it on.

He straddled his Harley and fired up the engine.

Crashing never sounded so exciting.

CHAPTER TWO

"Earth to Chloe. Pass the potatoes, pipsqueak."

Chloe gave her brother Jett a dirty look, but passed the bowl of scalloped potatoes as she did so.

Jett dipped out a healthy portion before handing the bowl to their foster brother, Zac.

Jett looked at her and shook his head. "Damn, girl. Where the hell are you today? I asked you three times to hand me those before you even heard me saying your name."

She shrugged. She'd been floundering around, lost in her own thoughts since running into Blake again at the studio on Thursday. Seeing him had brought up a whole bunch of feelings—sadness, regret, anger—as well as an unbearable mountain of lust. He'd been her first and, while she'd never admit as much to the asshole, there was some truth to that line about him ruining her for all other men.

While she'd taken her fair share of lovers, Blake had always been the yardstick she'd compared them to and none had measured up. Not even close.

Which pissed her off even more because hell would freeze over before Blake Mills touched her again, and she didn't care if that meant taking responsibility for every single one of her own orgasms from now until the end of time.

"Chloe!" This time it was Justin yelling her name.

"What?" She didn't bother to hide the irritation in her tone. Her annoying brothers could see she was distracted. Why didn't they just leave her alone?

"What's wrong?"

"For the last time, nothing."

Her mother tilted her head, studying her face. "This is about Blake, isn't it?"

The head of every sibling at the table flew up.

"Blake Mills?" Caliph asked.

She closed her eyes, wishing she were anywhere else right now. Seeing her first love had thrown her for a loop. There was no way she was ready to undergo the Spanish Inquisition about that unexpected reunion with her family. "He's one of the models for the Blessing House calendar." The Blessing House provided temporary housing for homeless families. Her mother had served on the board for years, organizing fundraiser after benefit auction after bake sale to keep the House open and solvent.

This year, the fundraising committee had decided to take a page from the book of other large cities, putting together a sexy calendar as a fun way to raise money. The calendar, "Hot Hunks in the Big Easy," was gathering a lot of attention, and given her mom's successful track record, was certain to make a slew of cash for the Blessing House.

Justin looked at Mama. "You're putting thugs in the calendar?"

Chloe grinned, appreciating his appalled tone. It was nice to know her brothers always had her back.

"No. We're not. Agnes Rogers found him. Apparently, Blake is a detective with the NOPD these days. She called me a couple of days ago to say the police department would be well represented."

"The hell you say," Jett proclaimed. "How hard up is the city for law enforcement? They're hiring crooks now?"

"Who is Blake Mills?" Caliph's girlfriend, Jennifer, asked. Jen and Caliph had started dating a few months earlier. Since then, she'd become a staple at the family's Sunday dinners. Chloe adored the woman and hoped she and Caliph would stick.

"Chloe's first boyfriend," Caliph answered. "A real badass and every father's worst nightmare when it comes to the guy you don't want your daughter dating."

"He wasn't that bad," Mama said. "I swear that poor boy's reputation has grown more despicable with every telling. Next thing I know, y'all will be swearing he was a serial killer and responsible for every hurricane to ever hit New Orleans."

Chloe sighed. Mama had never wavered in her belief that there was some good buried deep inside Blake. Right after she'd gotten off the phone with Mrs. Rogers, Mama had called Chloe to make sure she was okay with taking pictures of Blake. Chloe had assured her mother it wouldn't be any big deal, but she'd never managed to pull the wool over Mama's eyes and obviously she hadn't fooled her this time either.

Of course, since learning he'd joined the police force, her mother acted as if her faith in Blake had at last been proven true.

"We broke up when he stole money from Mama and took the silver serving platter my grandmother had given my parents as a wedding gift."

Jennifer winced. "Yikes. Doesn't sound like a very nice guy. And you say he's a cop now?"

Chloe nodded. "Yeah. And he's posing for the calendar."

Jennifer reached over and squeezed her hand gently. "That can't be easy for you. I know I wouldn't want to have to work with my ex on anything. Ever." Jennifer's ex-husband had left her for another woman. That painful event had led to her meeting Caliph. In an attempt to reinvent herself, Jennifer had shown up at Midnight Ink and gotten her first tattoo from Caliph. Since then, Chloe had watched her older brother fall head over heels in love with the woman. It was sweet. Even if it did reinforce the loneliness that had plagued Chloe lately.

She would be thirty on her next birthday, and while that age wasn't bothering her, it forced her to recognize some things she'd been ignoring. Like the fact she wanted kids. A slew of them like her mother had. Chloe absolutely adored her big family and she dreamed of having her own. But to do so, she had to get serious about dating and finding the man she wanted to marry. She'd put off doing that for too long, focusing instead on building a clientele for her photography studio and putting her book together.

"It'll be okay, Jennifer. I really only have to see him one more time. I'll snap a few pictures and walk away. No harm, no foul."

A quick glance at her mother's face proved her lie wasn't convincing the one person she really wanted to believe her.

Before she could reassure Mama she was speaking the truth, the doorbell rang.

"Chloe's the closest," Jett pointed out, not bothering to put his fork down as Zac snickered.

She rolled her eyes. They may all be adults, but there was something about returning to this house each Sunday that seemed to bring out the child each of them held on to. "Lazy jackass."

Jett gave her a shit-eating grin as she rose to answer

the door while they all continued eating.

She barely paid attention as she swung open the front door. It wasn't unusual for neighbors or friends to stop by on Sunday, as they knew the entire family would be there. Mama always made enough to feed an Army and as such, there was plenty of room at the large table for one or two or twelve drop-ins.

Chloe wasn't aware that her mouth had flown open until Blake placed his hand on her chin to push it closed.

"What the hell are you doing here?"

Blake smiled. "Mama Lewis invited me."

Chloe shook her head. "That's Mrs. Lewis to you and she wouldn't do that."

"Chloe," her mother called out from the dining room. "Invite him in."

Chloe closed her eyes, hoping that by blocking out Blake's cocky face, he'd simply vanish. When she opened them to find him still standing in the doorway, she muttered, "I'm going to kill her."

Blake chuckled. "If you do that, I'll have to pull out my handcuffs and arrest you."

She was tempted to slam the door in his face, then reconsidered as a wide smile crossed her face. Maybe this wasn't such a bad thing after all.

Blake's lowered brows betrayed his sudden suspicion

at her quick change in demeanor. "You like the idea of handcuffs?" He grinned, his dirty mind kicking in.

"No, perv, I don't." She was lying, but she wasn't about to admit her libido had suddenly jerked into gear at the thought. "You realize you're about to willingly walk into the lion's den, right? My brothers will tear you limb from limb."

Unfortunately her threat didn't faze the infuriating man. "I'm banking on your mother to protect me. But just in case," he patted his hip, drawing her attention to his holster, "I'm packing."

There was no way she could convince him to leave and time was up anyway. If she stalled much longer, her brothers' curiosity would win out and they'd all manage to make their way to the front door, lazy jackasses or not. She stepped aside, allowing Blake to enter.

He glanced around the entryway, looking fondly at the photographs and furniture. "It's exactly the way I remember it."

"Everyone is in the dining room and my food is getting cold." Her tone was short and annoyed, but she didn't feel like playing nice. He didn't deserve it. He'd hurt her worse than anyone in her life and while that wound had been inflicted nearly a decade earlier, it ached as if it had happened only yesterday.

She hated that she'd let him get so deep inside her he still had the power to cause her pain.

Blake waited for her to lead the way. She kept her eyes on her mother as they entered the room together. She didn't have to look at her brothers to see how pissed off they were.

Jett stood, his stance pure aggression. "What are you doing here?"

"I invited him," Mama replied, as if bringing the man who'd stolen from their family into their home was the most natural thing in the world. Of course, for their mother, it was. Her capacity for forgiveness was limitless.

Chloe could only assume that attribute skipped a generation because God knew she couldn't find it in herself right now.

Her mother rose, then gestured to an empty chair next to her as she grabbed a plate from the sideboard. "Help yourself, Blake."

He smiled his thanks as he took a seat. "I apologize for being late. Wound up pulling some overtime after the midnight shift. Lots of idiots on the street last night. Took me a few extra hours to finish the paperwork."

Chloe reclaimed her seat, grateful that Justin sat between her and Blake.

Blake kept his attention on her mother, pointedly ignoring the glares he was receiving from everyone else at the table. "I was sorry to hear about Papa Lewis."

Mama smiled gratefully. "Thank you, Blake. We all miss him something terrible."

That was an understatement, but Chloe didn't say anything. Though her father had passed away three years ago, sometimes it felt as if he was just away, working on the oil rig and that he'd be back, crashing through the front door with that loud bellow of his, telling all his kids to get their asses downstairs so he could hug them. Her father had been a giant of a man—Caliph and Jett had gotten his stature—but as gentle as a butterfly.

"And what is your father up to these days, Blake?" her mother asked.

Blake fell silent for only a moment, then gave her a rueful smile. "He's up to twelve months served on a twenty-year stint in prison."

"Oh, I see."

Blake shrugged. "Not surprised, are you?"

Mama shook her head. "Not really, but I *am* sorry."

"Don't be." Blake's voice was harder than Chloe had ever heard it. "I'm the one who put him there."

"You put your own father in jail?" Jennifer asked.

Blake looked at Jennifer, clearly waiting for an introduction. Caliph quickly did so. "This is my girlfriend, Jen."

Blake smiled. "Nice to meet you, and yeah, I did. He was selling drugs at some of the local schools. And not just marijuana, but ecstasy and heroin. I think there are a lot of people better off with him in jail."

Chloe put her fork down, unable to swallow through the lump that had grown in her throat. She knew Blake's childhood hadn't been easy, but he'd never shared many details about it with her. She hadn't known him at all until the summer he'd gotten a job at the sub place near the community college she attended. They'd both gone to different public schools, growing up on opposite ends of the city.

"I'm sorry, too," Chloe said softly. Blake caught her gaze, his eyes reflecting too many emotions to register—sadness, regret, anger, remorse. She looked away rather than face them. She'd seen all those things when they first met as well.

Maybe she was more like her mother than she realized—inexplicably drawn to people in pain, in need of rescue. Though Blake sure as hell hadn't let her save him. She doubted that would change now and she refused to be pulled back into Blake's life.

Jett broke the silence. "Guess the police force is a more interesting job than Sid's Sub Shop. Isn't that where you used to work?"

Blake nodded. "Yeah. Met Chloe there. She used to do homework between classes at the table in the corner." He faced her once more. "You still put down those Italian subs like you're never going to eat again?"

Her brothers chuckled. She flashed them all dirty looks until they sobered up.

Blake may be older, but the bad boy was still there,

lurking beneath his skin. She could see it in his face as he gave her a crooked grin.

It was the same smile that had captured her attention back in college. She'd taken one look at the bad boy behind the shop counter and fallen hard. A lot of people had tried to warn her away from him, telling her stories about how he stole beer and cigarettes from convenience stores, drove his motorcycle like he had a death wish and vandalized buildings. Blake had never denied the stories, but he'd never gotten caught either.

It hadn't mattered to her at the time because when he was with her, he had been sweet and funny. Her badass biker boyfriend. Given her goodie-goodie status, it had felt scandalous to be with someone with a reputation and wonderful to be so adored by him. She'd always hoped she had helped him be a better person, while he taught her how to be just a little bit wicked. Whatever they'd done for each other, there had never been a doubt in her mind that Blake had loved her.

Until he disappeared. Then she'd spent months—years—wondering what had been real and what had been lies. In the end, she'd felt used and stupid. And so angry.

"It was wonderful of you to volunteer to participate in the calendar." Her mom looked genuinely pleased and almost grateful.

Why was Chloe the only person who remembered the past?

Chloe snorted at her mother's praise, drawing

everyone's attention to her. "He drew the short straw."

Blake grinned, while Mama looked confused. "Short straw?"

Blake leaned back in his chair, looking far too comfortable and at home. "It's a good cause. I don't mind helping out."

Caliph rolled his eyes. "I'm sure you don't. As I recall, you don't have a bit of trouble strutting around with your shirt off."

Chloe gave Blake a superior smile, grateful for Caliph's snide comment. Finally. She'd warned him about her brothers' anger and though it would cost her in good karma, it felt good to watch them give Blake shit.

Blake crossed his arms, drawing too much attention to the muscles bulging beneath his t-shirt. "I figure those of us who haven't let ourselves go owe it to those who have to step forward. By the way, I don't remember seeing your name on the list of models, Caliph."

Caliph's eyes darkened as Jennifer slowly wrapped her hand around his wrist. Chloe was trying to decide if the touch was a warning or Jennifer's way of holding Caliph in his seat.

"I'm still trying to convince my sons to participate. We have two slots open." Mama gave Caliph a hopeful glance.

"I told you, Mama, I don't think the older members of your group would embrace the idea of a guy covered in tattoos."

Jennifer shook her head as if the argument was a familiar one. "I told him that only *every* woman who bought the calendar would be into that, but he's stubborn."

Caliph gave Jennifer a sweet kiss on the cheek. "Not every woman in the world is as open-minded as you, Jen. There are plenty out there who still turn up their noses when they see my ink. Besides, I have no desire to make a jackass of myself, posing like some king of *GQ*."

Mama looked from Caliph to Justin, but he cut her off at the pass. "Don't look at me. I already suckered Ned into doing it. You only need one marketing exec." Ned Kinnaman was Justin's partner at their advertising firm and one of the sexiest men Chloe had ever met. She was actually a bit nervous about photographing Ned. He literally oozed sex and sin.

Justin laughed when he spotted Chloe's flushed cheeks. "See," he pointed at her, making her blush even more. "That's what Ned's going to bring to the calendar. I've done my part."

Chloe scowled at her brother for embarrassing her, then she caught a glimpse of jealousy in Blake's gaze. Revenge reared its beautiful head.

"I'm not going to lie, Justin," she said as she fanned herself. "I'm really looking forward to Ned's day to pose. He's February, and I'm envisioning putting him on my bed with red silk sheets, completely naked, except for a box of chocolates covering his—"

"I think we get the gist," Justin said, cutting her off and pretending to shudder. "We don't need to hear the dirty details about your photo shoots with all those sexy bachelors. Good thing you're single. You can have some fun as you work." He winked at her, careful to make sure Blake couldn't see his face.

Chloe loved her oldest brother and his nose for mischief. She had absolutely no intention of posing Ned that way and Justin knew it, but that didn't mean he wouldn't help her get a few digs in at Blake.

"I didn't realize the photos were going to be risqué," Blake said.

Mama frowned. "Neither did I."

Oops. Chloe would have to tell her mom she was joking before she left today or she was liable to receive concerned phone calls from every woman on the fundraising committee tonight.

The rest of the meal passed much more easily than Chloe would have expected. Conversation turned to innocuous things as Justin described his latest project and Caliph and Jennifer talked about the long weekend trip they'd planned to take to Key West. Blake was a polite guest, answering questions about his work and complimenting her mother's cooking.

Once dessert and coffee had been consumed, the family began to rise. Jett and Justin made their goodbyes, both claiming to have other plans, while Zac, Jennifer and Caliph went to the living room to watch TV. Her mother was tidying the kitchen, which left Chloe alone with Blake.

Blake peered toward the kitchen door. "Let me pop into the kitchen to thank your mom and then I'm going to head out."

Chloe nodded as Blake disappeared into the kitchen. She walked to the front door to wait, anxious to see the frustrating man on his way. Her insides felt like churned butter and she was tempted to move Blake's photo shoot forward, simply so she could get it over with.

She cheered herself up with a mental pep talk. She'd meet him at Lake Pontchartrain—she had no intention of ever getting on his motorcycle again—take the pictures, then turn around and walk away. This time, it was Blake who was going to see taillights. The whole thing shouldn't take more than three or four hours. Surely she could survive that much more time in his presence.

"That's a deep thought."

She was startled by his voice, jumping slightly when she realized Blake was standing right next to her.

She put her hand on the doorknob, ready to get him the hell out of her mother's house, but paused. "Should I pat you down to make sure you aren't sneaking off with something?"

She felt horrible the moment the words crossed her lips, but there was something about seeing Blake again that was bringing out the worst in her. She didn't consider herself a bitter person by nature, but for days, all she'd been able to summon was cold, hard anger. Well, that…and lust.

Blake took her comment in stride, lifting his arms. "You won't hear any complaints from me. Take your time on that area below the waist. Lots of pockets down there."

She blew out an exasperated breath, though she was able to admit she'd walked right into that one. "Don't be such a pig."

"Hey, you're the one who offered. I've never looked a gift horse in the mouth. Should I turn around?" He spun, lifting his hands to the wall. The position sent her eyes straight to his ass, which he wiggled for her amusement.

One brief burst of laughter escaped before she could shut it down. Damn him. "Turn around and get out, you idiot."

"I love your laughter."

Chloe tried to ignore the tug his soft comment evoked. It had always been there between them—this electrical current that flowed hot and powerful, tying them together in ways Chloe could never understand…or fight. It was always sparks, heat, energy and painful need.

"Walk outside with me."

Blake had her hand in his before she could refuse. It appeared his take-no-prisoners attitude was still there as well. She'd followed his lead when she was nineteen because she was young and inexperienced. If he still thought she was that same silly girl who would come merely because he beckoned, he was destined for disappointment. She tried to pull her hand away, but his grip tightened.

They participated in a mini tug-of-war all the way to his motorcycle. Once they were there, he reached for a helmet. "Hop on."

She laughed at his audacity. "No."

"Get on the bike, Chloe. You need to get away for a little while. I can see it in your face. When is the last time you escaped, letting wind and the road take over until you forgot everything and everyone?"

Ten years ago.

She didn't say it aloud, but something in Blake's expression told him he knew the answer. "I'm not getting on the motorcycle with you. Not now. Not ever again."

"Yes, you will."

She narrowed her eyes. "Blake—"

"Our photo shoot, remember? We're taking the Harley to the lake."

"I have too much equipment. I'll follow you there in my car." She was pleased to see she'd stumped him with that. Clearly he hadn't taken that into account.

Blake leaned against his motorcycle casually. "So

what are your plans for the week?"

She shook her head at his audacity. "None of your business."

He lifted one shoulder at her dismissal. "Maybe. Maybe not. You taking pictures of the manhandler?"

Chloe felt an uneasy flutter in her stomach. Blake Mills on a mission was never a good thing. He had the tenacity of a pit bull when he wanted something. She'd always blamed that on the fact he'd basically had to raise himself, given his father's disinterest in his son and his lack of mother.

"Again, none of your business."

"Give me your phone."

"Why?"

Before she could stop him, Blake had one arm wrapped around her waist, the other diving into her back pocket. She placed her hands on his chest, intent on pushing him away, but the man was solid muscle, his chest rock hard. Once her phone was in his hand, he released her and took a step back. It bugged her that she hadn't been able to break free on her own.

He clicked the cell on, taking her to task for her lack of a passcode. He went to the contacts page and, as she watched, added his name and phone number.

"I'm deleting that."

"No. You're not. At least not until all of the calendar pictures have been taken. You're going to be alone with these guys and, while your mom and the committee might trust their characters, I'd feel better if you had my number handy. You feel threatened, even just a little, you call me. Okay?"

"I can take care of myself."

"Oh yeah?" Blake turned her phone off, grasping her once more. "Prove it."

"What?"

He slid her phone into her back pocket, taking advantage of the opportunity to run his fingers over her ass. She tried to shove him away, but she'd have had more luck moving a mountain.

"Break free from my hold and I'll delete the number myself." His arms tightened around her.

Chloe's mind whirled over all the self-defense moves her brothers had taught her when she became a teenager and got boobs. The more her body developed, the more intensive their training. "I don't want to hurt you." She put as much bravado into her tone as possible.

Blake laughed. "Of course you do."

She noticed he'd positioned himself so that his balls were protected and her bent arms were trapped against his chest. She marveled at how familiar, yet different Blake's body was. He'd always been tough as a young man, his body lean and fit, but now…

Chloe couldn't help but wonder what drove Blake to work out so much. Why did he need to be so damn strong? Blake had only shared skeletal notes of his childhood with her, never giving details. All she'd had to go on was his scant information, usually shared by accident, and her gut feelings. Yet, she'd always viewed him as a wounded beast, striking out at the world as a means of defense. Chloe had also thought she was safe from his swing, assumed she was different.

She'd learned the hard way how wrong she was.

"Don't, Blake."

His arms loosened slightly. "Don't what?"

"Don't set your sights on this. On us. It's not gonna happen."

He didn't move, continuing to hold her close. All of his attention, all of his focus homed in on her. She'd been the center of his universe for three glorious months. She remembered how special and wonderful that had been. Even so, it wasn't worth the inevitable pain that followed. She wouldn't play the fool for him again.

"I get it, Chloe. I'm sure you think I don't, but I do. If I were a better man, I'd accept that I hurt you, that you have every right in the world not to trust me and I'd keep my distance. You didn't deserve what I did to you and I'm not real sure how to make up for that. Maybe I can't. But the thing is, I'm going to try because I'm *not* a good man. I'm a selfish bastard. And I want you. I never stopped wanting you."

Chloe's lungs seized as she struggled for air. There was determination written on every line of his face, but more frightening than that was the hunger in his eyes. She'd seen it before—in the faces of the foster kids her mother had taken in over the years. The kids had always looked like they were starving to death, like they would do whatever it took to get a bite of bread. Chloe knew that hunger wasn't literal. What those kids—like Blake—wanted more than anything was love. Unconditional love.

"I can't give you what you want. Not the forgiveness. Not the understanding. And not the..." She couldn't say the word *love* to him. Couldn't let that single syllable out in his presence. "I'm not the girl I used to be." She wasn't sweet, trusting, or gullible anymore. He'd squashed those characteristics out of her, stomped on them until they simply vanished.

Blake released her waist. She had only a split second of freedom before he took her face in his hands. She wanted to shove him away, but she was rooted to the spot. "Yes. You are. You're still that girl and a hell of a lot more. But I'm more too. And I want a chance to prove that to you."

She started to shake her head, but Blake's grip tightened. "Blake—"

Her denial was cut off with a kiss. The second his lips touched hers, she was transported back in time. Their first kiss had been right here, in almost this exact same spot. They'd spent weeks circling around each other at the sub shop, her flirting while he made completely inappropriate but entirely hot sexual innuendoes. Then one afternoon, he'd offered her a ride on his motorcycle and she'd accepted. They had ridden around the city for nearly an hour as Chloe clung to his leather jacket and breathed in the humid Louisiana air. They'd stopped at the French Quarter, walking along the crowded streets until dusk, talking about everything and nothing. When he'd pulled up in front of her house that night, Blake had gotten off the Harley, taken her face in his hands and kissed her.

It had felt just like this—exciting, scary, overwhelming, powerful. And then—like now—Chloe had been helpless to do anything other than accept.

Helpless.

The word jarred, going through her like nails on a chalkboard.

She placed her hands on his shoulders and pushed. Blake clearly hadn't anticipated her refusal as he stepped back, slightly off balance at her rough shove.

"I'm going inside."

He smiled. "Running away isn't going to save you."

Her pride piqued. "I'm not running. I'm finished with the conversation. I'll text you later this week once I've found a place to take your photo for the calendar. We'll get it over with and then, this," she waved her hand between them, "is over. Again." She stressed the last word, letting it punctuate her sentence like an angry accusation.

Of course, Blake didn't acknowledge anything she'd said. "We'll see." Then straddled his bike, put his helmet on, fired up the engine and pulled away.

Chloe balled her hand into a fist, wishing she had something—anything—to punch. Blake infuriated her, pissed her off, left her struggling to keep her wits.

She released a loud "argh!" then muttered every bad name she could think of as she returned to the house. The front door had only just closed behind her when she heard her mother calling out for her to come to the kitchen.

She sighed. The kitchen window faced the front yard, which meant her mother had no doubt witnessed the entire scene with Blake. Great. Her Sunday just kept getting better and better.

"Did you need help with something?" Chloe asked, half-heartedly hoping for a reprieve. She didn't get it.

Her mother was sitting at the small kitchen table, sipping a cup of coffee and looking wearier than Chloe had ever seen her.

Mama shook her head, then pointed to the chair across from her.

Chloe decided to take the bull by the horns. There was no purpose to beating around the bush. "I guess you saw Blake kiss me."

Her mother didn't reply at first. "Actually, no. I didn't. I didn't think it was my place to spy."

Chloe bit her lip, wondering if there was any physical way to kick her own ass. "It didn't mean anything."

Her mother smiled, though the expression certainly didn't depict happiness. "Aren't you tired, Chloe?"

Chloe was. Exhausted. But she couldn't understand how her mother knew that. "What do you mean?"

"Anger takes a lot of energy to maintain. You've been holding on to your Blake fury for nearly a decade now. Doesn't that leave you drained?"

Chloe swallowed heavily. Truthfully, until running into Blake this week, she thought she'd let go of all those old hurts. If someone would have asked, Chloe would have laughed and sworn she didn't have any feelings for the man one way or the other. This past week had proven that belief false. She was harboring more pain and rage than she'd thought possible. And her mom was right. It was wearing her out…dragging her down.

"I was just surprised to see him again. It sort of knocked me back to a bad time. But it'll pass soon."

"No. It won't. None of this is going to go away until you forgive him."

Chloe's temper sparked. "Forgive him? God, Mama. At some point, you're going to have to stop being a doormat, stop letting people take advantage of your kindness."

"I don't think it makes me weak to try to find the good inside people. That's not being a doormat. It's being compassionate."

"And look what that compassion got you. Blake stole

two hundred dollars from your purse. That was our grocery money for the week. Maybe you don't remember how tight times were back then, but I do. We barely made it until payday at the end of the month."

Her mother reached into the pocket of her apron and pulled out a wad of money, tossing it onto the table between them.

"What's that?" Chloe asked.

"Blake just gave it to me. Five hundred dollars. To replace the money he stole and to make restitution for the platter."

"That doesn't cover it. Grandma Jeannette's platter was a family heirloom—irreplaceable. It was the only thing that survived the fire that destroyed everything your family owned. You were just sixteen and you lost everything. Everything except that platter. Maybe you think three hundred covers it, but I don't."

Mama sighed. "Chloe, you're not mad about the money or the platter."

Chloe wanted to deny it, but couldn't. In some ways, it was easier to maintain her fury over tangible things. That was simpler to explain to her mother. To herself. If she delved deeper, she'd have to admit to things she couldn't find the words to express.

"He said he loved me. Then he left without a word. Just disappeared for ten years. I guess in some ways he did me a favor. He taught me not to be such a sucker, not to believe everything someone tells me."

"Have you ever considered there might have been a good reason for his departure? Have you asked him why he left?"

Chloe shook her head. She wasn't interested in exploring ancient history. "It doesn't matter now."

Mama reached across the table and took her hand. "Of course it does. As long as this is hurting you, the reasons matter. It's time to swallow your pride, Chloe, time to put aside your anger and get some answers. Otherwise, I'm afraid you're destined to be tired for a very, very long time and I couldn't stand to see that."

"I'm sorry I called you a doormat. I didn't mean it."

Her mother grinned. "I know. Now…about this plan to have Ned posing nude…"

Chloe laughed, then spent the next hour reassuring her mother she and Justin were joking and that the calendar would be perfectly respectable.

CHAPTER THREE

Blake leaned against the wall of the building, watching the front door of the Blue Note. Chloe was inside the bar, taking photographs of one of New Orleans' most talented and lusted-over jazz musicians. He wanted to pretend he was here to simply keep an eye on her. After all, one of the men posing for the calendar had apparently tried to manhandle her, and while he knew Chloe was perfectly capable of taking care of herself, he figured it wouldn't hurt to be close by…just in case.

Unfortunately, he knew the truth. He was so jealous, he could hardly see straight.

He'd never been a possessive lover with any other woman in his life. The only one to ever evoke that emotion had been Chloe. He reached into his wallet and pulled out a tattered picture. He'd carried the photograph around with him for a decade—clinging to it like a lifeline through some of the darkest times of his life.

The image of Chloe, riding his back, piggyback-style, as the two of them mugged for the camera never failed to help him find his way. Though she wouldn't believe it, Chloe had helped him become the man he was today. She'd fallen in love with a boy who'd always thought himself unlovable. After all, his father declared him worthless on a daily basis and his mother had split when he was just six months old. From the day he'd been born, no one had ever looked at him the way Chloe had. Like he hung the moon. Like he was a hero. Like his life mattered.

So…whenever he got lost or started down the wrong path, he'd pull out this picture and clean up his act, find a better direction. He wouldn't be where he was today without her. Until he'd seen her again last week, he'd been content to maintain his distance because that was safer. For both of them.

He had considered looking her up the second his feet hit the pavement of New Orleans almost six years earlier. After he left her, Blake had spent four years on the road, the first couple with his father. Sometimes they traveled alone, other times, they would ride with a motorcycle gang. He'd done a lot of things he wasn't proud of during that time—petty thievery, vandalism, smoking pot and drinking heavily. He'd even participated in several fight clubs as a means of making money. He'd beaten up a few of his opponents badly, the images of their bloody faces haunting him too many nights.

However, he'd walked away from it all the night his father and a few of his friends cornered a waitress in a bar parking lot where they had all spent hours getting wasted.

Blake had sat with them, nursing the same whiskey, fed up with his life. He'd spent hours watching his father as the realization he was turning into his old man dawned hard. Looking at himself in the mirror behind the counter, he saw the same hard eyes, tight lines by his mouth and haggard expression. It was as if someone had dumped a cooler full of ice water over his head, forcing him to wake up, covering him with a freezing cold numbness that almost made his teeth chatter.

When his father threw the struggling waitress onto the hood of a car and started to lift her skirt, the other men holding her down and tearing off her clothes, his dead soul came to life. He didn't remember grabbing his father or pulling him away from the woman. There were only brief flashes of recollection in his memory. Of him pounding his old man into the asphalt. Of him beating the shit out of the other three men. Of the crying woman running away—her eyes reflecting absolute fear even though he'd just saved her. He didn't blame her for being afraid. He could only imagine what he'd looked like in that moment. Too many years' worth of rage had found their way to his fists and he was a man out of control.

In the end, all he recalled was standing in the middle of a dark parking lot with four unconscious men and the sound of sirens in the distance. He'd hopped on his bike and never looked back.

"Blake? What are you doing here?"

Blake blinked, forcing himself to the present, shocked to find Chloe standing in front of him. How the hell had she left the bar and walked all the way across the street without him noticing? So much for this stakeout.

Chloe looked completely annoyed. And a bit nervous.

He grinned. He could work with that. "I just got off duty, so I thought I'd take a little walk."

She rolled her eyes. "Not much of a walk. I could see you from the front window of the Blue Note. You've been holding up this wall for the last twenty minutes. How did you even know I was going to be here?"

"I'm a detective."

She smirked. "My mother told you."

He chuckled. "Yeah. I just wanted to make sure you were okay."

She sighed. "I'm perfectly capable of fending a guy off if he oversteps, despite my failed attempts with you."

He knew that, but he suspected she'd prefer thinking he was just concerned for her safety rather than the fact he was so jealous he couldn't see straight, so he let the lie stand. "Are you finished for the day?"

She shrugged. "I'm finished as far as working with Mr. January is concerned. Now I'm heading back to my studio to download the photos, find the best and tweak it."

"Have time for lunch?"

She hesitated, but didn't instantly refuse. Blake took that as a sign of progress. Before she could answer one way or the other, he pointed down Bourbon Street. "What do you say we grab some crawfish beignets at Bayou Burger?"

Chloe crinkled her nose. "Please tell me you don't still eat those."

Blake wrapped his arm around her shoulder, gently directing her toward the restaurant. Chloe fell into step easily beside him.

"Gotta say, Chloe, I'm sorry to hear you're still a finicky eater."

She scoffed. "The fact that I don't cover every meal in hot sauce does not mean I'm picky. Quite the opposite, actually. It means I prefer to taste my food. You should try it some time."

He laughed, the two of them trading barbs about their eating habits all the way to Bayou Burger. It wasn't until they were seated and their drinks ordered that Blake could lean back and relax without worrying she'd change her mind and run.

"It was good to see your family again on Sunday, but I'm not sure who Zac is."

Chloe took a sip from her water glass. "He's my foster brother. You wouldn't have met him. He came to live with us the summer after you…" She paused.

There was no point pretending. "After I left," he finished for her.

She nodded. "He and his younger brother, Noah, were removed from their home when their mother was arrested for prostitution and drugs. Zac was fifteen and Noah was only twelve. Before they came to stay with us, they'd been living in a house with no running water and eating whatever they could steal from dumpsters behind restaurants."

The story sounded familiar. Blake had done a bit of fine garbage dining himself when he was younger, but Chloe didn't know that. He'd never told her anything about his childhood because at the time, Blake had worried she would either dump him or worse, pity him. There were times he wished he could go back and kick his nineteen-year-old self's ass for being such a prideful idiot.

Listening to her tell Zac's story, he didn't hear sympathy as much as anger toward the boys' mother.

"How long did they stay with you?"

Chloe sighed. "Two years the first time. Then the court—in its less-than-infinite wisdom—gave them back to their mother. Their lives returned to more of the same, only worse. Their mother kept smoking crack and sleeping with men for drug money. One of the guys—a customer—beat Zac up one night. It was really bad. Noah was scared so he ran to a neighbor's house and called my mom. She phoned the police, then all three of my brothers. They got to the house just before the cops and found Zac in a bloody heap on the floor."

"Jesus." Blake couldn't imagine how hard it would have been for those young boys to spend two years in the loving, safe Lewis home, only to have to give that up to return to the slum. Then he recalled the few times he'd found security in his young life. Every single time, he'd willingly given it up and gone back to the hell that was life with his dad.

"Mama said she'd never been so scared in her life. She thought Zac was dead. Anyway, Caliph stayed with Zac, while Jett and Justin helped Mama and Noah pack up all their belongings."

"What about Zac and Noah's mother?"

"She'd been passed out in her bedroom. Didn't even realize anything had happened to Zac. She came out in the hall and started screaming at my mother because she thought she was stealing her sons. She told them to get out, to leave her boys alone. Justin said Mama looked that woman straight in the eye and told her she should be ashamed of herself."

Blake fiddled with his fork, chuckling. "Did it work?"

Chloe grinned. "What do you think? Mama's good at guilt trips. It's pretty much the way I was raised. She only had to look at me with that *I'm so disappointed* face and I'd crumble like a house of cards."

Blake laughed. "I remember that. She used that look on me a couple times. It's powerful."

"Justin said the lectures we'd gotten as kids were small potatoes compared to the speech she gave Zac and Noah's mom. He said he was nearly in tears and begging for forgiveness himself and he hadn't done anything wrong. Their mom fell apart when she saw Zac lying on the floor and she asked my mother to take her boys, to give them a chance to grow up safe and healthy. They've been ours ever since."

"What happened to their mom? Did she straighten her act out?"

Chloe shook her head sadly. "She's still alive. I know Zac goes to see her every now and then, takes her some food and medicine, but no. There wasn't a happy ending. She's still addicted. You know how that goes."

Blake knew only too well. "Yeah, I do."

"Did you really arrest your dad?"

He nodded. He'd been expecting the question ever since he stupidly made that comment at Sunday dinner. "I did."

"That couldn't have been easy."

Blake shrugged as he recalled the near-rape in the bar parking lot. In some ways, putting his dad in prison had been a hell of a lot simpler than he would have thought. "My dad and I had parted ways several years before the arrest. He'd been a criminal, on some level, for my entire life. Stealing, drunk driving arrests, drugs—selling and using—assault, you name it, it was on his rap sheet."

"Why didn't you ever tell me that when we were dating?"

Blake wasn't pleased with his answer, but it was the only one he had. "Pride."

She frowned. "What?"

He released a long breath. "You weren't like any other girl I'd ever dated, Chloe. You didn't come from the same place I did. When I was with you, I could pretend I wasn't that guy."

"What guy?"

"My life wasn't all that different from Zac and Noah's. Only I was dealing with a drunk dad instead of a strung-out mother."

"I wish…"

Chloe's whisper faded away, leaving Blake to fill in the blank. What did she wish? That she'd known? That Mama Lewis had shown up in the middle of the night and dragged *him* out of hell? That he hadn't been such a prideful, puffed-up idiot?

He smiled. "There are a lot of things I wish too. But none of that matters. I've done a lot of things I regret, Chloe, but I can't let my mind linger on that too long. Everything that's happened has made me the man I am today."

She studied his face in silence, glancing away briefly. Then her eyes lifted to his once more. They were shuttered, closed and he knew she was finished with this conversation.

The waiter brought their meals and they allowed the conversation to drift to safer realms. Chloe talked about her experiences putting together her book and he shared some of his more humorous arrest stories just so he could hear Chloe's laughter.

Once he'd paid the bill, he took her hand, offering to walk her back to her place. She didn't refuse.

When they arrived, she invited him inside, giving him a tour. The studio apartment was a large, wide-open space, filled with sunlight and color. It suited Chloe perfectly. Near the front door, she'd set up her portrait area with lighting and backdrops, tripods and cameras. Then, they walked farther into the room to her living area. A plush couch and ottoman flanked by two recliners all faced the large-screen television.

Blake whistled. "Damn. Man cave."

She laughed. "Yeah. My brothers and I are huge hockey fans and I was tired of all of us trying to cram ourselves into Jett's shoebox apartment on game nights."

"Why not go to Justin's? Didn't he mention something on Sunday about his house?"

Chloe nodded. "Yeah, but he lives too far out of town. The trek there and back in a cab is a pain. And Caliph's work schedule changes all the time."

"So you put a hockey haven in your apartment."

She grinned. "Yep. Between October and April, you can find at least a couple Lewises here almost every night, depending on the match-ups."

"Sounds like fun. I'm a Maple Leaf fan myself."

Chloe looked horrified. "Dear God. I didn't think anyone rooted for Toronto unless they were forced to because they lived there. You must be a glutton for punishment."

He narrowed his eyes. "They aren't that bad."

She shuddered, clearly enjoying the opportunity to push his buttons. "Yeah, well, they aren't that good, either."

"You and I are going to make a wager once the season starts back up."

"What makes you think you're still going to be around come October?"

Blake reached for her before she could read his intent. He tugged her body flush against his until he could feel her hot breath on his face. "I'm going to be here."

She opened her mouth to chastise him, but there was only one way he'd accept her tongue-lashing and that was literally. He kissed her, holding tightly—partly out of fear she'd try to stop him and partly because there was no way he could resist the feeling of her body pressed against his. The last decade melted away—all the pain, anger and loneliness fading until there was nothing left, but this moment. And them.

Chloe wrapped her hands around his neck, the action

lifting her breasts higher against his chest, capturing his attention. Keeping one arm around her waist, he brought his left hand up to cup her breast.

Chloe's lips left his as she released a sharp, excited breath. Blake increased the pressure of this touch, squeezing, kneading. Neither of them sought to continue the kiss. Instead, Blake placed his lips to her forehead as Chloe panted softly, her quiet mews encouraging him. He ran his hands under her shirt, savoring the softness of her skin. He stroked his way around her waist, up her sides until he found the breast he'd just left. He smiled when he felt her lacy bra, the texture reminding him of the first time he'd ventured under Chloe's shirt. Her breasts were slightly smaller then.

However, Chloe's response was just the same. Her breathing was heavy, her body so hot, he wondered how she wasn't burning his fingers. Her hips—now, like then—ground against his, taunting his cock, driving him insane with need.

When he was younger, he'd insisted they were made for each other. Chloe would laugh and tease him, claiming it was the girl's job to be the silly romantic, not the guy's. However, after years spent trying to find warmth in the arms of too many women, he realized it hadn't been a foolish dream. It was the truth.

Blake ran his hands along the top of her bra, enjoying the slight shudder his touch provoked. Then he dipped his fingers beneath the lace, delving deeper until he found what he was searching for.

"God!" Chloe jerked when he lightly pinched her nipple, but his arm was still wrapped around her back and it kept her from escaping. Not that she was trying to. She plunged her hands into his hair, gripping it so tightly it stung. He didn't care. He relished the pain, loved feeling her passion, her need. It made him feel less alone.

He pinched her nipple again, firmer this time. Chloe's hips thrust against his and he wished there weren't so many damn clothes between them.

That thought prompted action. He reached for the button on her jeans, delighted when Chloe mimicked the motion on his pants.

"I want you, Chloe," he whispered, needing to make sure she understood. If they took their pants off, he was lying her down on the couch and taking her.

"Hurry up."

Her words hit him like the loud bang of a starter pistol. The only sounds in the room were those of the rushed flurry of hands as they unzipped and tugged down their jeans, of shoes hitting the floor, of a foil condom wrapper crinkling and Chloe's soft cry when Blake lay her down on the couch and came over her. He pushed his cock deep inside her with one hard thrust.

It wasn't until he was completely buried that they paused, both of them panting, air being sucked in and blown out loudly. Blake rested on his elbows above her, studying her flushed face, her closed eyes.

"Chloe. Look at me."

Her eyelids flittered open, her vision clearly fuzzy. He waited until her focus returned. He saw the moment it happened because a crease formed in her brow. They'd acted on impulse, neither of them considering the consequences of what they were doing until now.

Blake's heart raced and his jaw clenched as he resisted the overwhelming need to thrust, to pound, to fuck.

"I won't be another regret."

She frowned. "What?"

"I know you regret what happened between us all those years ago and I wish there was some way I could go back in time and change what I did, but I can't. I can't undo the hurt, Chloe. Can't fix the mistakes."

"Blake—"

"But I'm telling you right now, I can't be another regret in your life. If that's what this is going to be, say so and I'll stop."

She didn't speak for several tense moments. Blake held his tongue, gave her time to decide while silently praying he'd have the strength to leave her if that was what she asked.

Finally, she cupped his cheek in her hand. "I don't want you to stop."

It was all he needed to hear. He lifted his hips until

his cock was just barely inside her, then slid in again. She wrapped her legs around his hips as his thrusts grew harder, went deeper. Chloe worked free the buttons on his shirt, not bothering to remove it. She simply slid her hands beneath the cotton, her nails scratching their way along the muscles of his shoulders and back. She'd left her mark the first time he'd taken her too.

Chloe may have been the virgin when they succumbed to this passion ten years earlier, but she'd been the one to teach him. About burning, heart-pounding lust. About craving. About giving and taking and what it truly meant to be hungry. He may have spent too many nights with an empty belly as a child, but until Chloe, he'd never suffered genuine hunger.

And he'd never experienced sex mixed with love until her. Hell, he hadn't felt it since.

Not until now.

Chloe's hips lifted to meet his and her soft groans told him exactly how close she was. He reached down, intent on drawing more than just one orgasm from her. He'd spent years dreaming of having her under him once again. He wasn't going to waste the opportunity.

He pressed her clit firmly, loving the wild, unrestrained response it provoked. Chloe's back arched as she released a loud cry. He thought he'd loved the sound of her laughter, but that music was a far second place. Blake waited a few seconds as Chloe trembled, her climax running its course. Then he fired the trigger again. He stroked her clit as he increased the speed of his thrusts.

Chloe gasped, shaking her head. "I can't. Not again. Too much."

He kissed her roughly, cutting off her refusal. He knew her too well to be fooled by such a lie. They'd spent a summer in each other's arms. He remembered exactly how many times she could come in a night and they weren't even close to that number yet.

His kiss combined with his finger on her clit and his cock pounding inside her hot pussy pushed her over the edge a second time. This time, he didn't stop moving, working instead to draw the sensations out, prolonging the pleasure for her.

As the orgasm subsided, Chloe's arms left his shoulders, dropping heavily to the couch cushions beside her. Her eyes were closed—her face the perfect blend of exhaustion and bliss.

"We're not finished."

She blinked rapidly, forcing her gaze to his. "I'm out of shape. It's been a few months since…"

Blake laughed. "It's been almost two years for me. So get your second wind. There's no way I'm letting this end so fast."

"Years?" Her skeptical expression was flattering…and slightly insulting.

He narrowed his eyes. "Yeah. Just so we're clear on this, I'm not some sex-craved pervert sleeping in a different bed every night. I do have standards."

Chloe shook her head in mock disappointment, laughing softly. "Damn. Such a shame. What happened to the horny, gets-hard-when-a-strong-wind-blows bad boy I fell in love with all those years ago?"

He knew she meant her words as a joke, but all he could focus on was the reminder that she used to love him. He'd thrown that away because of pride and stubbornness. "A week ago, I would have said he was gone, but now…"

Blake punctuated the pause with a quick, hard thrust. Chloe gasped, her arousal firing hot once more.

She tightened her legs around his waist. "Do that again."

He tilted his head, considering. He'd never taken the submissive role in the bedroom and he didn't intend to now. He held still as Chloe worked hard, trying to force him to move. She lifted her hips as much as her position underneath him would allow. When that failed, she dug her heels into his back, trying to push him as low as she could.

When all her attempts proved fruitless, she stopped moving and gave him a dirty look. "You joined the police force and yet, you still suck at following commands."

He chuckled, kissing her lightly on the cheek. A decade apart hadn't changed one thing. It still felt as if Chloe knew him better than he knew himself. "I'm a model detective. But doing my job there and doing it here are two entirely different things. Put your hands above your head."

"Why?"

He lifted one eyebrow, letting his impatient look answer the question. She lifted her arms, resting her hands in a position of surrender. It turned him on. A fact that wasn't lost on Chloe as his cock twitched and grew even harder.

She sighed. "Liar." The word wasn't spoken with malice or accusation, but he was confused by the name. Then she added, "You are still a very bad boy."

He grinned, pleased, then bent his head to take one of her nipples into his mouth. They hadn't shed a damn piece of clothing besides their pants—something he would rectify the next time—so he added extra pressure, sucking harder, making sure she felt his touch through her blouse and bra.

Her back arched as she attempted to keep his mouth there. He added his teeth to the game, nipping lightly at first, then digging deeper.

She cried out, not in pain, but in true pleasure.

He lifted his head. "And you're still trying to pretend you're a good girl."

She cupped his face with one of her hands, intent on pushing him back to her breast. Blake gripped her wrist firmly, pressing it against the couch cushion above her head. "Don't move your hands or I'll tie you up. I have my handcuffs with me."

Her pussy clenched tightly against his cock. Blake

fought to restrain a groan, stars forming behind his eyelids. Chloe had liked it rough; her sexual needs a mirror image of his. At nineteen, he'd chalked it up to her innocence, believing her desires were fueled by genuine curiosity. Now he knew it was more than that. Not all women were created equal.

Blake pushed off his elbows, grasping Chloe's wrists in his hands, forcing them into the cushion. The power play, the show of strength had Chloe's eyes drifting closed, her body shuddering with need.

"Please, Blake." Her voice was soft. He knew what she was asking for.

He withdrew from her body until just the tip of his cock remained and then he shoved in hard, going as deep as their bodies would allow. Chloe didn't shy away from his almost brutal thrusting. Instead, she added her own fuel to the flames, joining the rhythm, driving her hips up as he came down. The only sound in the room was that of their mingled cries and the slapping noise of skin on skin. Blake's grip on her wrists slipped a bit as both of them started to perspire, the temperature in the studio rising to rival that of the sun.

Neither of them stopped for air or for rest. Instead they kept fighting for climax, two bodies slamming together in a selfish search for completion. Chloe came first…and second. Two orgasms, one right on the heels of the other. She groaned loudly, trembling, but when Blake refused to give way, to stop, she quickly recovered, rejoining the race.

When he finally approached his end, Blake released one of her wrists, letting his fingers drift along her body to her clit. He wanted to feel her coming around him again as he found his own pleasure.

Chloe jerked when he touched the swollen, sensitive nub. "I can't," she cried.

He stroked her clit faster. "Yes, you can. You're going to come with me, Chloe. You and me. Together."

She gasped and he felt the familiar fluttering of her pussy. She was almost there. Thank God. Blake was seconds away from falling over the cliff himself. Chloe pushed him off. Her inner muscles clenched, squeezing his cock almost painfully. He dropped to his elbows as he came, jet after jet of come filling the condom.

"God." The word felt as if it was ripped from his chest. Every muscle in his body tensed in beautiful agony. How much time had passed since he'd been this affected by sex? He knew the answer to that.

Ten years ago.

Chloe lay beneath Blake, refusing to open her eyes. She'd told him she wouldn't regret it.

But she'd lied. And not for the reasons he might think.

Chloe had done some serious introspection since the conversation with her mother. She'd comprehended the wisdom in her mama's advice. Chloe needed closure where Blake was concerned.

She'd had her heart broken by him when she was young, inexperienced, foolish. As a result, she'd held on to that pain, harbored it, made it larger than it should have been. She was an adult now, a woman, and she was no stranger to love affairs or casual sex.

Chloe believed if she slept with him just once more, she'd realize she had built him up to some mythological proportions that were inaccurate. A brief, one-time fling with Blake would prove to her that he was a man just like any other and she'd be able to let go of her sex-god beliefs and move the hell on.

So much for that idea.

"Closing your eyes isn't going to make me disappear." Blake's smug voice proved he knew she was trying to hide from the consequences of her actions.

She didn't open her eyes. "Maybe you'll think I fell asleep and leave peacefully."

He kissed her cheek. She wished that friendly, platonic buss didn't feel so freaking good. "I'm not leaving."

He was still buried inside her, his body covering hers in such a warm shelter, she found it hard to remember why this was wrong.

Chloe released a long breath, then let her gaze find his. He was more handsome now than he'd been at nineteen. Though he'd never had a boyish look, not even when he was younger, some of the hard lines around his mouth and eyes had softened.

"You don't look as pissed off at the world as you used to."

Blake chuckled, unoffended by her remark. "People don't annoy me as much these days."

She needed to get away from him—put some distance between them before she said or did something else completely stupid. Chloe lightly pressed on his shoulders, surprised when he gave way easily. He sat, helping her up as well. He made no move to stop her when she rose and began to tug on her jeans. Mercifully, they'd limited the disrobing to just the waist down.

Blake stood as well, walking to her kitchenette to throw the condom away before tugging his own pants on. Because of the open floor plan of her apartment, the only area of the place closed off by walls was the bathroom. She had placed a large Chinese screen at the foot of her bed to give the illusion of a bedroom and to hide the fact she had a tendency to leave her dirty clothes lying in a heap on the floor.

She followed him to the kitchen, feeling some of her confidence return now that she was dressed again. Chloe opened the fridge and pulled out a couple of bottles of water. She tossed one to Blake, suddenly aware that he hadn't bothered to button his jeans or shirt back up. They both hung open in a way that was far too sexy for her peace of mind.

She reached up to her hair. She'd started the day with a loose ponytail, but most of it had escaped the elastic band. She felt around, trying to find the band, intent on repairing the mess.

Blake took a long swig of water then crossed the room, taking her in his arms. He reached up and tugged her hands down. "Leave it. You look tousled and sexy."

"Blake." She needed distance.

"What do you say for the encore we take all our clothes off and try to make it to your bed?"

She scowled. Cocky, arrogant asshole. "Actually, you can take the rest of that water to go. I have work to do. Thanks for the trip down memory lane. It was fun."

Chloe hoped she'd infused just the right amount of dismissal and hell-will-freeze-over-before-we-fuck-again into her tone.

Apparently she had because Blake's brows furrowed. "You think that was a one-night stand?"

"It might be more accurate to say it was a one-afternoon stand."

Blake shook his head. "Think again."

He hadn't released her. Instead, he'd tightened his grip, letting her feel just how much he wasn't finished with her yet. How in the hell could he be hard again already? Then she considered the foolishness of her thought. This was Blake. The more things changed, the more they stayed the same. He'd always been ready to roll when it came to sex.

She wanted to hate his alpha power plays, wanted to be pissed off by them. And in a lot of ways, she was. Unfortunately, they also triggered some latent desire to be completely dominated by him. Not in everyday life—that would drive her nuts and force her to cut his penis off.

But in the bedroom…sexually…God yes.

Before she could respond, the door to her apartment slid open. Justin and Ned walked in. Chloe tried to push Blake away, but he held fast.

"Let go of me," she muttered when she caught her older brother's dark look.

"You heard her," Justin said, his fists clenched. Great. Nothing like adding embarrassment to mistake.

She'd been wrong to think she could open the door a crack for Blake and not expect him to push it wide and walk in.

Justin's gaze took in her messy hair and Blake's open shirt, his scowl growing. It was far too obvious what had taken place here.

Time for distraction. She shrugged out of Blake's arms, flushing hotly when he reached down to zip up his jeans, not bothering to hide the action from her brother and his business partner. "What are you doing here, Justin?"

"You and Ned have an appointment to discuss the calendar, remember? We had a work meeting on this side of town, so I rode with him, figured I'd chill on your couch while the two of you worked out a plan for Ned's pose."

Ned grinned, obviously sensing her desire to diffuse the volatile situation. "He was planning to be a pain in the ass, making me regret volunteering to do this damn thing. If it had been anyone other than Mama Lewis asking, I would have said no."

Chloe smiled gratefully. "I'm sorry. I forgot about the meeting. Give me a second to…" To what? What was she supposed to do now? Blake didn't look like he was going to go peacefully.

Justin crossed his arms, letting her know he was going to watch her every move. She shot him a dirty look, then turned to Blake.

"I really do need to get back to work."

"What are you doing for dinner tomorrow night?"

She rolled her eyes. He was like a dog with a bone. "Listen, Blake. We tried the relationship thing once and it failed…miserably."

"We were kids, Chloe. That hardly counts as a serious attempt."

He was right, but that didn't mean the way things ended hadn't hurt. A lot. "I'm nothing like the girl I used to be."

"So we'll go out for dinner, get reacquainted."

"Looks like you already did that," Justin muttered.

She turned around. "Dammit, Justin. Mind your own business."

Blake buttoned his shirt. He leaned closer, keeping his ultimatum quiet enough only she could hear it. "I'll go as soon as you agree to dinner."

"That's blackmail," she whispered.

He didn't reply. Just gave her that wicked, bad-boy grin that always got her into trouble.

"Fine. But just dinner. Nothing else—not a movie or dancing or coffee at my place afterwards. And I'm meeting you at the restaurant. No riding together."

Blake looked like he might argue, but she raised her hand to cut him off. "Those are my conditions. Take it or leave it."

"Fine. I'll call you later with the details."

She shook her head. "Just text me." Until she gathered her wits about her, she wasn't about to get roped into another conversation with him. Texting was safer.

Blake nodded, then kissed her, the touch too fucking familiar and sexy when his tongue brushed hers.

She half-heartedly pushed at his shoulders. She was about to get the mother of all ass-chewings from her brother. Of course, that was a given. So…she might as well get her money's worth. She felt Blake's brief spark of surprise when her tongue entered his mouth and she gave his ass a quick squeeze before she stepped away.

"Goodbye, Blake," she said, proud of the strength in her voice.

He grinned. "I'll talk to you later."

Justin didn't bother to step out of the way as Blake left. The two men faced each other like adversaries on the battlefield and for a moment, Chloe thought she might have let her guard down prematurely.

Then Blake stepped around her brother, leaving without another word. Chloe released a long breath when Blake slid the door closed behind him.

"Does somebody want to confirm that's who I think it is?" Ned asked.

Ned Stevens had been Justin's best friend since their freshman year in college. They were assigned as dorm roommates and they'd been inseparable ever since. In truth, Ned had become a member of the family, another damn overprotective brother. Just what Chloe needed.

"My old boyfriend, Blake," she answered, realizing the simplicity of the answer would never satisfy either man.

"Are you sure he's not a current one?" Ned asked with a wicked grin.

"What the hell was that, Chloe?" Justin threw his

hands up in disbelief. She didn't blame him. She'd been pretty cold to Blake at Sunday dinner. Now, forty-eight hours later, she was boinking the guy on her couch.

"I don't know what that was."

"The guy's a thief," Justin added.

"He gave Mama the money back on Sunday." Chloe wasn't sure why she was saying that as if it forgave all. She certainly hadn't felt that way two days ago.

"Oh. Did he tell you why he took it and ran off?"

Chloe shook her head. "No. I didn't ask."

"Why not?"

She couldn't explain why she hadn't asked Blake. Not even to herself. The question had been on the tip of her tongue every single time she'd seen him since his return, but something always caused the words to get lodged in her throat. "What difference would it make, Justin? We know he did it. Can you think of a good reason why he would steal Mama's money and disappear without a trace for nearly a decade?"

Justin considered the question briefly, and then shook his head. "No, I can't. Which is why I don't understand your reason for playing hide the salami with the guy again."

She blew out an annoyed breath. "Don't be such a juvenile."

Her brother grinned, used to her admonishing him for his colorful, somewhat vulgar nicknames for sex. Justin wrapped his arm around her shoulder, pulling her close and placing a sweet kiss on her forehead. "Just be careful, pipsqueak. Maybe the guy has changed. But maybe he hasn't. Keep your eyes open this time. Okay?"

She nodded. Eyes open was her initial intent. Then Blake had fucked her into a state of delicious delirium and she'd allowed it to blind her once more.

"So, tell Ned all about this idea you had for him, a bed, a box of chocolates and no clothes."

Ned crossed his arms and scowled. "I told you, Justin, I'm not doing that."

Justin's face reflected pure mischief as he ignored his friend's complaint. "And listen, Chloe, don't waste a bunch of money on the big heart-shaped box. A small sampler will be more than enough to cover his—"

Justin didn't get to finish his joke as Ned punched him in the arm.

Chloe laughed, grateful for their timely interruption and the welcome distraction. She spent the next hour plotting with Ned over possible locales and poses, while Justin cracked jokes at both of their expenses and made a general nuisance of himself.

It was exactly what she needed.

For now, it was her turn to escape.

CHAPTER FOUR

Chloe had postponed her dinner date with Blake, putting him off for four straight nights. She hadn't intended to skip out on him, but she'd been knocked down by a killer case of the flu. The illness had put her in bed for two days before she graduated to resting on the couch for two more. As a result, she was days behind on her shooting schedule and scrambling to make up for it.

Blake had offered several times to take care of her, but she'd refused, claiming she didn't want him to catch what she had. Even so, that hadn't stopped him from making little deliveries outside her apartment door. One day, he'd left flowers, the next a quart of homemade chicken soup. Two days ago, she'd found an erotic romance novel. Inside Blake had written an inscription, telling her he hoped it would inspire her for the next time they went out. All it had done was leave her hot and bothered. And she'd been too worn out to use her vibrator to nip the problem in the bud. She'd read him the riot act for that after he called to see if she'd gotten his gift. Asshole had just chuckled and told her to hurry up and get better.

Chloe ran a comb through her damp hair and sighed. She'd gotten a shower first thing this morning, hoping it would wake her up and give her some sort of energy. She was tired of being…well…tired.

She dragged herself to the kitchen counter, fired up the coffeepot, then sat down to look at her calendar. If the models could be a bit flexible with their schedules, perhaps she could double up on shoots and still hit the publishing company's deadline. She hated missing deadlines and refused to see the fundraiser lose even a single dollar due to her illness.

She picked up her cell and for the next hour, rearranged everything until she managed to fit in every single model. While Chloe was laid up in bed, her mother had managed to find guys for the last two months, so they had a full year's worth of hotness ready to roll. All Chloe had to do now was dash from one end of New Orleans to the other every day, then spend her nights choosing the best photo for each month and enhancing it.

She looked at her schedule. Eleven photo shoots and twelve portraits to touch up in less than two weeks. She was screwed.

Her phone rang. She glanced at the number and sighed. Her last model. Blake was the only man who hadn't answered when she'd called. "Hey, Blake."

"Back in the land of the living?"

He'd called her every day since their impromptu hook-up on Tuesday afternoon. It was strange how easily they'd fallen into familiar patterns. Blake called her as soon as he got off duty and then again before bedtime. Their conversations had only touched on safe subjects—like their jobs, the weather, sports—but they'd become the highlight of each day for her.

She hadn't questioned him about his disappearing act ten years earlier and they never addressed what his return in her life meant.

"Yeah," she replied. "I'm back and sort of wishing I could crawl under the covers and hide again. There's no way I'm going to hit this calendar deadline."

Blake didn't sound concerned. "Of course you can. I'm around if you need help."

"Uh, thanks, but no thanks. I tried to give you some photography lessons a long time ago. All you managed to master was dark and blurry."

Blake chuckled. "That was before I got my iPhone 5. Now I take great pictures."

Chloe groaned.

"Besides, I wasn't offering to take the photographs, just to lug your equipment, help you set up the shoots, stuff like that."

"And you're doing this all out of the goodness of

your heart and not because you want to play chaperone while I'm taking pictures of the shirtless, hot guys, right?"

"Absolutely." His tone was pure innocence, but she knew him better than that.

"Forget it. You'd just clam jam me." She restrained her giggle at the silence that followed her comment, then he gave into curiosity.

"I give," he said. "What the hell is a clam jam?"

"Female equivalent of a cock block."

Blake snorted with laughter. "God. There is something seriously twisted and wrong with you. I blame it on all those brothers you grew up with."

She leaned back in her chair, propping her feet up on the one across from her. She was smiling and happy for the first time in days. In less than five minutes, Blake had found a way to make the stress she was feeling over her work vanish and the tension in her shoulders subsided.

"So I see I missed your call. You putting off our date again?"

She had called him for that reason. "Yeah, I'm sorry. I'm wicked busy."

"I understand."

"Hey listen, I need to try to find a time to do your photo shoot. Are you still determined to take the pictures on your Harley by the lake?"

"Yep. And you're riding with me."

"I told you, Blake, my equipment—"

"Downsize it as much as you can. I borrowed a big-ass motorcycle bag from a friend of mine. We can put your cameras and stuff in there."

"What if it rains? My equipment costs—"

He cut her off. "It's waterproof."

"Why do you want me to get on that bike again so badly?"

"Why are you so resistant?"

Chloe wasn't sure how to answer. They'd spent that entire summer so long ago on his motorcycle. It was the last time she'd felt carefree, wild, over-the-moon happy. He'd also driven off into the sunset on that motorcycle. While it wasn't logical, it was easier to forgive Blake, the cop, the man who didn't exist all those years ago, and hold on to her anger toward his bad-boy biker persona.

"I just don't think they're safe."

Blake snorted at her obvious lie. "What day did you leave open for me?"

"Let me see. I'm popping over to Justin's office this afternoon to take the pictures of Ned."

"No box of chocolates in bed?"

Chloe thought she detected the slightest trace of

relief in Blake's voice. "He wouldn't go for that. The most he would agree to was an open shirt with a tie hanging around his neck. We thought it would look cool if he was sitting at the head of a conference table. Set it up for today because none of the employees will be in the office since it's a Saturday."

"Sounds very tasteful."

No doubt she and Justin had given him a bad impression of what the calendar was about. Truth was all the pictures would be PG with none of the men exposing more than their chests and arms. Her musician had been sitting sideways on his piano bench, shirtless, in a vest and simple black pants as he toyed with a couple of keys. While she'd selected the shot she wanted to use, she'd come down with the flu before she could tweak the print.

"It's going to be a classy calendar."

"Of mimbos," he added.

She frowned, then a light went on. "You were eavesdropping on my phone call with Mama that first day."

"Yep."

She grinned wickedly. "Well, if you're expecting me to take it back or revise my opinion, I won't."

Blake chuckled. "You will. Eventually. I'll make sure of it."

His deeply spoken threat was laced with just a hint of

sexual malice. Chloe grew wet and warm at the thought of it. She pressed her legs together, suddenly annoyed at the way Blake could turn her into a raving sex maniac in mere seconds.

"In fact, what are you wearing right now?"

Chloe wanted to ignore his question, but that damn dirty book he'd given her had fired up some needs she really wanted taken care off. She hadn't bothered to get dressed after her shower, just donning her robe.

She decided to play hard to get. "Why do you want to know?"

"Tell me, Chloe."

"Just a robe."

"Nothing under it?"

She shook her head, trying to ignore how hot his questions were making her. "Nothing."

"Slip it open, but keep it on."

Chloe rested her phone between her shoulder and head as she untied the belt around her robe.

She heard Blake chuckle softly. "There's this feature on cells called speakerphone. Turn it on and put your phone down where you can still hear me. You're going to need both hands."

"Blake," she started.

"Just do it."

"Where are you?" she asked, suddenly worried about him initiating phone sex with her in the middle of the precinct.

"I'm at home. On my couch. Just got off-duty."

She turned the speakerphone on and placed the cell on the table. "Okay."

"Where are you in your apartment?"

"My kitchen table."

"Nice. I want you to do what I tell you. Follow my instructions completely. If I suspect you're cheating, I'll come over there, toss you over my knee, and paint your ass red with my hand until you learn to obey."

The feminist part of her was outraged and tempted to hang up on him, but, at the moment, her libido was currently making all decisions.

Blake appeared to have interpreted her silence correctly. "We both want the same thing right now." His voice sounded more distant. Apparently he'd put her on speakerphone as well.

"What are you doing now?" she asked.

"Unzipping my jeans."

She licked her lips, sorry she hadn't suggested postponing her meeting with Ned and inviting Blake over.

Before she could make the offer, Blake took charge. "Cup your breasts. Lift them up and squeeze them."

Chloe dragged her hands along her stomach, surprised by the sudden sensitivity of her skin. How could Blake get her to this point with no more than a few words? She held her breasts, her nipples budded, ready.

"Squeeze them hard. There's no point in denying you don't like your pleasure laced with pain."

Her face flushed, the response caused by embarrassment and need. She'd tried to hide her darker kinks from other lovers, always feeling slightly strange for her desires. She'd never had to do that with Blake. He'd just seen what she wanted and given it to her. No questions, no qualms. Hell, most of the time it seemed as if he wanted it even more than she did. Something she didn't think possible.

She applied the pressure to her breasts, pinching her nipples roughly. Her breathing grew heavier.

"Are you touching your nipples?" he asked.

"Yes," she whispered.

"Pinch them hard. Let me hear that pretty whimper of yours."

She tightened her fingers, suddenly self-conscious of her sounds.

Blake's voice when he spoke again, seemed breathless. "You can take more pain. Stop holding back."

She gave in to the desire, pinching her nipples harder than she'd ever dared. The sharp sting sent zings of pure pulsing arousal straight to her pussy. She pressed her legs together to capture the heat and moisture.

"Are you wet, Chloe?"

"God." She felt lightheaded with need. "Yes."

"I'm so hard right now. My hand is wrapped around my cock, but it's not the same as being inside you."

"Come over." The invitation was out before she could consider why she shouldn't issue it.

"I can't. You have to go to work soon. We're just going to have to let this be enough for now."

This was nowhere near enough. Chloe fought to restrain her brief flash of temper, a disposition her mother said she'd inherited from Papa Lewis. Like her father, she was prone to impatience and while their tempers ran hot, they usually only blazed hot for a moment before they were able to rein it back in. "Dammit, Blake."

"Shh. It's time to get serious. Keep one hand on your breast, while you drop the other lower. I want you to tell me how hot and wet your pussy is for me."

She obeyed his request, opening her legs. She drew her fingers along the seam, gasping at the sensations provoked by that simple touch. "Oh," she cried.

"You sound so sexy, Chloe. God, baby, you have no idea what you're doing to me. The head of my cock is seeping come and my balls are tight. We're going to have to move fast. I'm not sure how much longer I can hold off."

The gruffness of his voice told her he was telling the truth. Chloe wasn't worried. It wouldn't take much to push her over at this point.

"Rub your clit. Push your fingers against it hard and fast."

Chloe did as he asked. She groaned then released her breast, using her free hand to grasp the edge of the kitchen table. She needed something to hold on to, to keep her grounded.

"My cock is going to explode. Are you close?"

"Yes," she hissed, her fingers familiar with this motion. She was no stranger to masturbation and she knew all too well how to get herself off. Even so, this was way faster and so much hotter than anything she'd ever done. Knowing Blake was on the other end of the phone, imagining his hand stroking his own cock, his head thrown back against his couch with his eyes closed. It was as if he was sitting right in front of her, each of them performing their shows in person.

"Push two fingers into that hot cunt. Shove them in deep and fast."

Chloe knew what would happen if she did that. Her climax would be inevitable.

"Do it. Now, Chloe."

She pressed her fingers deep, thrusting them, pretending it was Blake's cock that was pounding inside her.

"Add another finger, baby. Make it bigger, thicker."

She obeyed, not bothering to slow her rhythm. She released the table and added her other hand to the game, fingering her clit, touching that one spot…that one place that made her…

She cried out loudly. "Oh my God. Blake." Chloe doubled over, her head flying toward her lap as her orgasm racked her frame. It was potent, powerful. Overwhelming.

She could tell from Blake's rough grunts that he was with her. She closed her eyes, letting herself see the jets of come erupting from his cock, landing on his shirt as the stroking of his hand slowed.

For several long moments, the phone line was quiet except for the soft sound of Blake's breathing. He was obviously listening to the same thing from her.

"You still there, baby?"

She grinned, dragging her fingers from her body, struggling to sit upright once more. "I'm going to need another shower."

He chuckled. "Wish I was there to scrub your back."

"That's all you'd scrub?"

"You ready to go again? So soon?"

She groaned at the thought. If he were here, she'd definitely give it the college try, but the truth was she was zapped. While the flu had passed, she suspected she was still a few days away from full-strength. "No. Unfortunately, I'm not."

He seemed to understand. "I'll take a rain check for the shower."

Damn man kept making these grand assumptions about their future. Granted, her actions weren't helping to dissuade him. Even so, she still had too much pride for her own good.

"You may be waiting a damn long time to collect on that. I'm still not planning to see you after the photo shoot."

Blake wasn't deterred. "You will. So when are we meeting to take the pictures?"

She glanced at the clock. She really did need to shower and dress then gather up her stuff for the shoot with Ned. She was in serious danger of being late. "What does tomorrow look like?" She hadn't scheduled anything for Sunday, pretending it was so she wouldn't miss Sunday dinner. Now that she was asking, she knew it was because she'd intended to give Sunday to him.

"I'm on-duty."

Chloe tried to ignore her disappointment.

"But I'm off next Sunday."

So it would be another whole week before she saw him again. Silently, she chastised herself. What was wrong with her? She was supposed to be over Blake Mills, not counting the minutes until she saw him again.

She tried to chalk up her weakness to the flu. Clearly she was still sick and not thinking clearly. "How about next Sunday afternoon after dinner at Mama's then? We're usually finished eating by two, so we'll have a few hours of good light."

"Is that an invitation to dinner?" he asked.

"Are you sure you really want to push your luck and step into the lion's den again?"

"Mama Lewis will protect me. She likes me."

Chloe wanted to deny that, but he was right. Her mother had always had a soft spot for Blake. Chloe blamed it on her Mama's tendency to root for the underdog.

"You know the drill. Table is loaded with food by noon. Get there by then or we're starting without you."

Chloe clicked off without saying goodbye, hoping that would make it clear she didn't want to see him between now and then. She rolled her eyes.

Sure you don't.

There was no way to ignore how excited she was about next Sunday.

By the following Friday, Chloe was regretting agreeing to help out with her mother's damn calendar even more than before. If she never saw another shirtless, beefcake, prima donna asshole again in her life, it would be too soon. With the exception of Ned—whose photo shoot was a blast—and a lovely pediatrician, the last five guys had run the gamut from God's gift to women to more demanding than J. Lo on tour.

Today's shoot was the one she'd been dreading the most. With good reason. The manhandler had arrived in full-force.

Javier Ramsey was one of New Orleans' premiere chefs, his restaurant in the French Quarter winning national acclaim from all the critics and making it a local hotspot whenever the rich and famous came to town. Reservations for dinner were booked months in advance.

Now Chloe was beginning to understand why he was so talented. It appeared he had at least a dozen extra hands, all of them managing to touch her constantly, and while his supposedly glancing blows hadn't crossed the line to inappropriateness yet, he was getting damn close.

Chloe reached up to adjust the lighting once more. Even though she'd told Javier to stand still so she could get it right, the man was behind her in an instant. He placed one hand on her hip as the other met hers on the light. His bare chest pressed against her back and she stifled the urge to curse. Their close proximity drew her attention to his erect cock.

Great. This wasn't going to end well.

Javier had elected to wear just an apron, and while she knew he had boxers on beneath it, they wouldn't appear in the picture. It was the most risqué portrait she'd done thus far and she was a little bit worried about her mother's response when she saw it. Of course, none of that would matter if Mr. Hands didn't stand still long enough for her to snap his picture.

"Javier," she said, her temper beginning to pique despite her attempt to remain calm. She'd been trying to set things up for nearly forty-five minutes, but Javier kept changing his mind about his pose. It was mid-morning and she wondered how long he could continue to stall before he'd have to give in and let her take the damn picture. The restaurant was opening in a few hours.

During their initial meeting, he'd sat too close to her on her couch as they'd discussed their ideas for the calendar. He had asked her out, but she'd refused. Then he'd played the French card, kissing her on both cheeks as he left. That wouldn't have bothered her if he hadn't lingered on the second kiss and placed it a bit to close to her earlobe, adding a bit of hot breath to the touch.

The guy squicked her out. Majorly. He'd called a few times since then, but she'd sent him straight to voicemail.

"I don't want you to burn yourself," he murmured, his lips too close to her ear for comfort.

She tried to take a step away, but he tightened his grip on her hip.

"I really need you to stand over there so I can make

sure the direction is correct."

"You are a very beautiful woman, Chloe."

She sighed and wondered how much it would piss her mother off if she brought her heel down on Javier's foot and crushed all of his toes. Given his behavior, she suspected her mother would encourage it. However, she recalled the fundraiser committee's glee when the famous chef had agreed to participate. They'd been thrilled, claiming his presence alone would sell tons of calendars.

"Thank you," she replied through gritted teeth. "I think the lighting is fine now. You can take your place." She didn't give a shit if his whole face was in shadow. She was snapping a few shots and getting the hell out of here.

Javier didn't appear anxious to move away, but mercifully, his sous chef arrived, an Amazonian woman named Elise whom Chloe had liked the moment they'd met. Javier released her and moved back to his place by the chopping board.

"What do you want?" he barked at his assistant, clearly annoyed by the interruption.

The woman must have been accustomed to his rude manner. "If we're going to serve the *tarte au pistou* tonight, I need to begin preparing the ingredients before the rest of the staff arrives."

"We're not finished yet. You'll have to wait. Go away."

Elise seemed unfazed by her boss's anger. She walked

over to Chloe. "How much longer will you be?" While her question was innocuous, the concerned look on Elise's face proved the woman was really wondering if she was okay.

Chloe tried to decide if there was any way she could finish her job without making a scene. Perhaps Elise could help. She handed the woman her phone and spoke quietly, hoping Javier couldn't overhear. "Do you mind clicking on my contacts, calling Blake Mills and telling him that I'm running late for our meeting. Tell him it would save time if he could meet me here."

"Of course." Elise gave her a subtle wink—all too aware that Chloe was calling in the cavalry—and took the phone out into the main restaurant.

Blake was at work and they didn't have any meeting scheduled. Hopefully he'd catch the drift that Chloe needed help and he'd come over. She wasn't all that worried about Javier trying something. Chloe was more than capable of fending off an overzealous womanizer. The problem was Javier wasn't responding to her verbal warnings. All she had left was her right hook. If she pulled that out, he'd withdraw his agreement to participate.

Chloe sucked at peaceful resolutions. She'd grown up in a houseful of boys. All disputes were handled quickly and efficiently…physically. While her brothers had never lifted a hand to hurt her when they were all kids, that hadn't kept them from wrestling or tickling her into submission in order to get a toy or the last dessert.

Javier started to walk back toward her, but Chloe

threw her hand up to halt him. "No, don't move. The lighting is perfect and I don't want to lose my shot."

The spotlight was nowhere near right, but it was close enough. Javier seemed to struggle for a reason to approach her. Failing that, he returned to his original place. She adjusted the camera lens, tweaking the focus and the aperture. She also awaited the inevitable. They'd gotten this far in the process three times before and each time, Javier had declared the pose wrong for some asinine reason or another. The only thing giving her hope was that the man was beginning to run out of places in the kitchen to stand.

Sure enough, just as she bent to click a shot, Javier threw up his hands. "This feels too awkward. I would never stand like this while cooking."

Chloe took a deep breath and counted to ten before speaking. "You aren't cooking. You're posing for a calendar. The idea of this shot isn't to show you working, but to capture you in your workplace. You're the one who chose to take the picture in the kitchen. Trust me. This pose is the best. Now hold still."

She plastered a fake smile on her face and decided if the asshole wanted to continue to bitch, he'd have to do so while she snapped away. She started clicking despite Javier's refusal to pose properly. If the bastard thought he was going to blow this shoot and drag her back here again for another attempt, he was sorely mistaken. She'd give money out of her own pocket to send in another photographer. She knew a couple of large, no-nonsense male colleagues who would be only too happy to do her a favor.

Chloe pretended Javier was doing a great job, even though she could see from his tight expression he was trying to come up with a way to stall. "Those are great. Now, what if you pick up one of the kitchen utensils? Grab that silver bowl. Maybe you'd feel better using props."

Javier hesitated, but Chloe kept snapping. Maybe the gods would take mercy on her and one of the shots would actually look good.

"Perhaps you could show me what you mean."

It was a deliberate attempt to draw her closer. Chloe wasn't biting. "You're the cooking expert. I'm just the photographer. I'm going to switch lenses. Just find a way that feels comfortable and natural." Chloe bent to grab the lens, intent on making the change as quickly as possible.

When she looked at him once more, Javier was grinning, his pose perfect. Hallelujah. The guy must have caught her hint. She focused and started to snap.

She'd only taken a few pictures when Javier turned around, pretending to reach for a pan hanging from a rack behind him. Chloe took two more pictures before her finger caught up with her brain.

"Where the hell are your boxers?"

Javier glanced over his shoulder, his slimy smile wide. "You said comfortable and natural."

"That's not what I meant." Chloe's head was beginning to pound, her patience officially gone.

"It would be easier if you came over here and posed me the way you wanted."

Chloe opened her mouth to inform the idiot the only way this would be easier was if he had a fucking brain, but at that moment, she was saved.

"Hey, Chloe. Whoa," Blake said, stopping mid-step. "Thought this calendar was PG."

Elise hovered just behind Blake. She giggled when she caught sight of her boss's bare ass.

"This is a closed photo shoot," Javier said furiously as he turned back around, the apron mercifully covering something Chloe *really* didn't want to see.

"I'm going to go adjust the menu. There's no way we're going to get the tarts made today." Before she left, Elise glanced at Blake, then gave Chloe an impressed look that said she approved of the cavalry.

Blake walked over to Chloe and gave her a quick kiss on the cheek. "I'm going to stick around. I'm Chloe's assistant."

Javier's face went red with frustration and fury. "I'm not comfortable working with another man in the room."

"I can see why," Blake murmured.

Chloe wavered between laughing hysterically and

crying her eyes out. She'd been running a hundred miles an hour since recovering from the flu. Now she was starting to think a relapse of the illness would be a welcome respite.

"Have your assistant wait outside." Javier drew out the word *assistant* to prove he wasn't buying Blake's lie.

Blake tucked a stray hair behind her ear before cupping her cheeks in his hands. The action was one of pure possessiveness. He didn't speak as he studied her face. She wasn't sure what he saw there. Probably because there were too many things to see. Chloe was tired, frustrated and, if she was being completely honest, somewhat amused by Javier's ridiculous antics now that Blake was here and she felt safe.

Mercifully, Blake didn't pick a fight with Javier. Instead, he made it clear that Chloe was spoken for.

Even though technically, she wasn't.

"Take your pictures, Chloe. I'll be right outside. How much longer do you need?"

Chloe glanced at Javier and saw the man's narrowed eyes. The chef didn't like discovering she wasn't available.

Even though technically, she was.

"Five minutes." It would be a miracle if she got a useable shot in that amount of time, but she didn't trust herself alone with the asshat chef for one second longer than that.

"There's no way we can finish in five—"

Blake cut off Javier's complaint. "I'll be back here in five minutes to help you pack up your stuff."

"But—" Javier blustered.

Blake tugged his phone out of his back pocket. "I'll make a few calls while I wait."

"Thanks, Blake."

Blake walked out of the kitchen, but from the clomping of his boots, she could tell he hadn't taken two steps into the other room before he stopped.

"Is that your boyfriend?" Javier asked. "I thought you said you weren't seeing anyone."

Foolishly, she had made that comment at their first meeting. She could only assume that was what had triggered open season on Chloe for the guy.

She glanced over her shoulder, certain Blake had remained within listening distance. She'd love to lie and say he was her boyfriend, simply to get the octopus off her back. But, knowing Blake, he'd find some way to make her repay him for that deceit. Probably with sex.

And with that thought, her libido reared its ugly head, assuring her it was a price it was more than willing to pay. It figured the one man who turned her into a raving sex maniac was also the one who'd broken her heart…and her trust.

Chloe simply nodded in response to Javier's question. Maybe that would cool his engines and Blake would be none-the-wiser about her pretending he was her boyfriend.

"Yes what? Yes, you're seeing him or yes, you aren't seeing anyone?"

"Javier, I don't see why my personal life has any bearing on this photo shoot. I'm here to take your picture for this calendar and that's it. Now, if you would just put your boxers back on and pick up that whisk, I could—"

Javier was across the room in three long strides. He grasped her shoulders tightly, tugging her against his chest. When he spoke, his voice was quiet enough that Chloe knew he understood how close Blake was as well. "You must know how much I want you, Chloe."

"Let go of me, Javier. I'm really, *really* not interested."

The chef paused and Chloe got the sense he was confused.

"Hasn't anyone ever said no to you before?" she asked.

He chuckled, the sound husky and deep. "Don't be ridiculous. Of course not."

His answer—so completely cocky—made her laugh. Javier released her, joining in her mirth.

She placed her hands in her front pockets. "Wow. You really are something."

"And yet, you're not interested?"

She shook her head. "Sorry."

"Not nearly as much as I am. Your boyfriend is a very lucky man."

For the first time, Chloe could see why other women would be attracted to the chef. After all, he was rich and famous, and attractive in a tall, boyishly handsome way. He rubbed elbows with Hollywood elite as well as international royalty. And he could cook.

However, none of that was even remotely appealing to her. Her ideal man had dark hair and crystal-blue eyes with a muscular body that wouldn't stop. He had a charming smile, wicked wit and a tattoo on his upper left arm.

She made herself stop listing attributes. She was describing Blake. Dammit.

"Our time appears to be running out. Shall we try to get in a good shot before your *assistant* returns?"

Chloe nodded, relieved when Javier tugged his boxers on—though he kept his back turned toward her—making a show of it. Then he turned on the charm for the camera, posing as if he'd walked straight off the pages of *GQ*. Of all her models thus far, Javier was the most natural, knowing how to highlight his gorgeous features to perfection.

Chloe had only snapped about two dozen shots when Blake returned, but she wasn't worried. She could probably fill the entire calendar with just the last few pictures of Javier and the thing would sell.

Blake didn't speak immediately. Chloe wondered if he could sense the tide had turned. She flipped through the images on her viewfinder and, satisfied with the results, she looked at Javier and smiled. "All set."

Javier reached for his pants and shirt as Blake helped her pack up all of her equipment. Given the end result, she felt guilty for calling him. Though she suspected Javier wouldn't have backed off if he hadn't seen Blake in the flesh. And really, if the chef had touched her one more time, there was no force on earth that would have kept her from cold-cocking the guy. Then Blake would have been called in anyway…to arrest her for assault.

"Sorry for bothering you when you were on duty."

Blake folded the legs on her tripod. "No problem. I actually wasn't far from here, working on a case. I'd just finished interviewing a witness and was heading back to the precinct to type up the report. Your timing was perfect."

Blake had told her a little bit about the details of his job. She wondered how he could stand to spend so much of his day dealing with anger and sadness and pain. He investigated cases involving domestic violence, child abuse and rape.

Javier walked over to say goodbye when they finished packing up. He gave Chloe two platonic kisses on the cheek, then—to her dismay—told Blake he was a very lucky man. Blake didn't bother to correct him. Instead, he gave her a wink that told her she was in his debt.

That didn't bug her as much as she might have expected.

Chloe retrieved her cell phone from Elise, thanked her for her help and she and Blake stepped out into the bright sunshine together.

"What's next on your list for today?" Blake asked as he placed her bags in the trunk of her car.

"I'm taking pictures of Caliph. At the tattoo parlor."

Blake chuckled. "Sounds like your mom wore him down."

"I think it was actually a tag-team effort. Jennifer was fairly convincing too."

"Guess I don't have to worry about your safety with your brother around. That's a shame. I was enjoying being your bodyguard."

"I shouldn't have called you, but I was dangerously close to pulverizing that guy, which would have pissed my mother off. I thought maybe if you showed up and I pretended that you were…" She wasn't sure why it was hard for her to say "boyfriend" to him, but for some reason, it felt wrong.

"Your boyfriend," he finished for her.

She nodded. "I thought that would make him back

off and it worked. So I owe you one."

Blake reached for her. Chloe didn't bother stepping away. Not when she wanted him to hold her. She was beginning to crave his kisses more than chocolate and that was saying something. "I think I like having you in my debt."

She narrowed her eyes. "I wouldn't call this a debt. Just one friend owing another a favor. A very small favor."

Blake placed his lips against her cheek, the touch more caress than kiss. His breath was warm against her skin, sexy and sweet, all at the same time. "When can I collect my favor?"

Her eyes had drifted closed, but now she opened them, her gaze taking in the busy street behind them.

What was she doing? Blake Mills had stolen from her family, broken her heart, left without a trace for years and now she was letting him walk right back into her life without so much as a hi or bye. She was letting her body make the decisions—choosing sex over common sense.

She took a step away. Blake looked as if he'd try to pull her back, so she added another step, more distance. "I can't do this again."

"Do what?"

She pointed to herself, then him. "This. Us. I've been down this road before and it didn't end well."

"I'm not the same man I was when I was nineteen

years old, Chloe."

"Why did you leave?" The words fell out unbidden, unwanted. Chloe hadn't meant to ask because she didn't want to know. In her mind, there was no reason good enough for him to do what he'd done. None.

Blake ran a hand through his dark hair. In the sunlight, it was so black it shimmered like water. It betrayed the Italian heritage on his mother's side, which was actually the only thing Chloe knew about Blake's mother apart from the fact she hadn't been around when he grew up.

"I was wondering when you were going to ask me that."

"Forget it. It doesn't matter."

Blake frowned. "Of course it does." Before he could say anything more, Blake's cell phone beeped. He read the screen and sighed. "I have to go. Domestic dispute. The neighbor just called it in."

She nodded. "Okay. I'm late for my shoot with Caliph anyway."

"I want to talk about this, Chloe."

She walked toward the driver's side door and opened it. "I meant what I said. You and I are ancient history, Blake. I think it would be best if we just left all of this in the past and got back to life as normal."

"I'm not going to do that."

She gave him a sad smile. "I wasn't asking."

Blake's eyes darkened with a determination that told her she wouldn't win this fight. "I'll be at Mama Lewis's house on Sunday for dinner."

Fuck. The photo shoot. "I have a friend who is a photographer. She's really—"

"No. You're taking the pictures."

"Blake. Please. Why can't you just let this go?"

He walked toward her, cornering her. "I made a mistake, Chloe. Shit, I've fucked up a million times. But if I let you walk away right now, without explaining, without fighting for you, it'll be the biggest mistake of my life."

He took advantage of the fact her mouth had fallen open. Blake's lips landed on hers, kissing her roughly, telling her in no uncertain terms that *this* was nowhere near over.

CHAPTER FIVE

Blake loaded Chloe's equipment into the motorcycle bag he'd borrowed from a friend as she watched, quiet and tense. She'd been the same way all through her family's Sunday dinner. Her mother had even remarked on her silence, but Chloe simply dismissed it, saying she hadn't slept well the night before.

Blake had followed her to her apartment on his Harley, refusing to budge when Chloe insisted she could drive herself to the lake. They were evenly matched on stubbornness, so Blake pulled out the "you owe me one" card, forcing her to give in.

He turned to find her on the sidewalk, her arms crossed stiffly. Blake tapped her on the nose, hoping the playful gesture would help her loosen up. "You're not facing the firing squad here. We're just going for a ride on my Harley, taking some pictures and having a little talk."

Her shoulders slumped slightly as she released a sigh. "Fine. You're right. Today's conversation is about ten years overdue. Let's get this over with."

Blake swallowed heavily as he considered what he'd say. They'd only dated for three months all those years ago. When he thought of it that way, it blew him away. Those ninety days had had a huge impact on his life.

Problem was he'd been a jackass when he was younger, too embarrassed by his home life to come clean to his pretty little girlfriend. He'd painted a picture of some badass guy who went through life with no regard for following rules or obeying authority figures. It was easier to pretend he didn't care what anyone thought of him than admit to Chloe how much he wanted her to look at him and see someone who was worthy of her love and respect.

He placed a helmet on Chloe's head, helping her with the strap before putting on his own. Then he threw his leg over the bike and gestured for her to hop on. The second her thighs rested against his, Blake felt himself transported back to the first time they'd ridden together. He'd watched her and her friends studying in the back corner of the sub shop where he worked for several weeks, his gaze constantly drawn to her bright blue eyes and her loud, infectious laugh.

Most of the time, Blake lived in a rundown apartment on the wrong side of town. That was whenever his dad didn't drink the rent money. During bad times, they crashed on the dirty floors of neighbors or even on the street. There weren't too many happy people in his world and Blake felt as if he were constantly wading through a sea of misery.

Chloe was the complete opposite of all that. She was light and sunshine and fresh air and laughter—all rolled into one beautiful package.

Blake fired up the engine on his Harley, loving the way Chloe leaned into him, pressing her breasts against his back. He weaved his way carefully through city traffic, glad when they hit Interstate 10. Blake pointed the nose of the bike toward the west and pulled back on the throttle.

Blake was never more at peace than when he was on his motorcycle. Sometimes it felt as if the roar of the engine was the only thing that could drown out his bad memories. He'd recognized that the first time he straddled a Harley. The feeling of peace the bike gave him hadn't waned since.

Chloe's grip tightened around his waist, but he didn't give way, didn't slow down. He knew her, knew she loved this feeling of flying as much as he did. It was another way they were alike, in synch. Sometimes it amazed him how many similarities he and Chloe shared, given their completely different upbringings.

For nearly an hour, it was just the two of them, soaking up the sunshine and the silence while letting the wind blow all the hurt away. Blake didn't pretend that pain wouldn't resurface, that the next few hours wouldn't be difficult. He'd never talked about his past or his father. Ever. But complete honesty was the only chance he had at possibly regaining Chloe's trust. And maybe even her love.

He'd bare his soul to the world if it meant getting her back.

Once they turned on Old 51 Highway, the traffic all but disappeared and soon, they arrived. Blake parked in such a way that Chloe could capture him and the bike with the picturesque view in the background.

She studied his choice and nodded approvingly. "This will work."

She removed the helmet and started to retrieve her equipment from the bag. Glancing up at the sky, then back at him, she gestured toward the sun. "We'll have to work fast in order to take advantage of the light."

He helped her set up the tripod, then moved the bike a couple inches this way or that as she tried to line up the perfect shot. Once she had the position she wanted, she pointed to his shirt. "Some guys have taken their shirts off completely, others have just unbuttoned them and left them hanging open. The musician wore an open vest with his jeans. It's up to you. Whatever your comfortable with."

Blake stripped off his shirt without hesitation. With his chest bare, the badge he'd hung from his jeans showed better. They'd discussed whether or not he should wear his gun belt, but decided against it.

Chloe rolled her eyes at his quick disrobing.

"You didn't really expect me to be shy, did you?"

She shook her head, then bent down to fiddle with her camera. Blake was unnerved by her continued silence.

Apart from discussing the photo shoot, she hadn't engaged in any real conversation. He'd let her get away with that until their work was finished. After that, all bets were off.

She snapped a couple of shots she called testers then nodded approvingly at whatever she saw in the viewfinder. "The crash point on this setup is amazing."

"Crash point?"

"Sorry. Photography slang. It's just an expression someone used in one of my classes once that stuck with me. Basically, it has to do with symmetry and the rule of thirds. You are the crash point. Everything in this image draws the viewer's eye to you."

She didn't bother to explain further. Instead, he stood, turning this way and that as Chloe worked her magic with the camera. He was no stranger to being her model. He'd posed for countless pictures that summer so long ago. She had been enrolled in her first photography class and was obsessed with applying everything she'd learned, dragging him along any time she needed a model.

Then he considered her term. *They* were at a crash point. Everything that had happened in their pasts had put them on this course, until now…all that was left was this moment and the truth.

Blake tried to put all that away, focusing on Chloe's instructions, letting her call the shots. He teased her about it, saying he'd never noticed her dominatrix tendencies. She pretended to crack a whip, then continued to take pictures.

All too soon, she decided she'd captured exactly what she needed. She appeared pleased, but that look passed quickly, replaced by one of reticence, nervousness.

Once they'd finished packing all the equipment away, Blake locked the bag, securing it to the bike.

"Walk with me." He held out his hand.

Chloe hesitated and he feared she'd refuse. He raised his eyebrows, silently pleading with her to give him a chance to explain.

She sighed. "Okay."

She accepted his proffered hand and they walked along the shore, listening to the sound of the water repetitively slapping against the bank. It was quiet for a Sunday afternoon in May. The weatherman had forecasted a late-day shower, so Blake could only assume the threat of impending weather had kept most people away.

He led her to a private spot then gestured at the grass. "Wanna sit down for a while?"

She nodded and plopped down on the soft ground. He joined her and they looked out over the lake.

Crash point, Blake thought once more. It was time. "You asked me why I left. I didn't have a chance to answer."

Chloe turned her head, looking back the way they'd come. He'd become very good at reading body language during his years on the force. Every fiber of Chloe wanted to run, to escape. But—in typical fashion—his brave woman resisted the urge. She faced him once more.

"So tell me."

"You are the most beautiful woman I've ever met, Chloe."

She rolled her eyes, clearly thinking he intended to charm his way out of answering.

"I mean it. When you grow up the way I did, well, let's just say, I wasn't all that familiar with women who smiled and laughed and were so genuinely honest."

A crease formed in Chloe's brow. "You never told me about your childhood. You just said you lived with your dad."

He nodded. "Do you know why I volunteered to pose for this calendar?"

She gave him an impish grin. "Because you drew the short straw?"

"I spent one Christmas in the Blessing House. A social worker found me and my dad living on the street. It was one of those rare, cold-ass winters in New Orleans. She told us about the house, said we could go there for the holiday. My dad told the woman to mind her own business. Actually, I think his exact words were 'Fuck off, bitch' but she didn't listen to him. She just handed me a flyer with the address to the house. Promised me I'd be warm and there'd even be presents."

"How old were you?"

Now that he'd opened the vault to his past, Blake found too many memories coming at him too fast. Maybe that was good. He could keep the emotions at bay because there wasn't time to process them. "Eleven. After she left, my dad fell into a bottle of whiskey and passed out. It was cold as shit that night. So, I covered my old man up with my blanket and walked nearly two miles in the dark until I found the address of the Blessing House. I'd been lied to by nearly every adult I'd ever met, so when I knocked on the door, I was more than ready to run in case it was a trap."

"A trap?"

He shrugged. "My dad wasn't the most law-abiding citizen. He'd taught me at a young age to always be on the lookout for the law."

"He told you the police were the bad guys?"

Blake nodded.

"And yet you joined the force."

He grinned sadly. "It seemed like the best way to stick it to my old man. The guy was a fucking asshole in case you haven't figured that out yet."

Chloe didn't reply. His words had come out too bitter, too strong. Most folks would have accepted that at face value. She didn't. "He was still your dad."

"I know. I spent one night in the Blessing House,

watching all the other kids—some with folks, some without—and in the morning, there was a present for me and I got a holiday meal."

"Sounds nicer than the street."

Blake lifted one shoulder. "I guess. I didn't stick around. I left the toy I'd gotten—some plastic fire truck—stole a bunch of food from the kitchen and a couple of blankets and took off."

"You went to find your dad."

Blake picked up a blade of grass, pressing it between his thumb and forefinger. "Yeah. I got worried about him being hungry."

Blake looked out over the lake. He hated trudging up all this old shit. It didn't change anything. His jaw tensed as he fought to beat back the anger. After several deep breaths, he was able to center himself again.

Chloe didn't seek to fill the silence with questions. She let him find his way through the story at his own pace. He appreciated that she didn't push him for more.

"I always took care of him. He was an alcoholic. He couldn't hold down a job for more than a few days at a time."

"So you became the caregiver."

He nodded. "Yeah. I guess so."

"It was the same for Zac and Noah. They kept the

house as clean as they could while their mom was strung out. Zac made sure Noah did his homework, got something for dinner, put him in bed at a reasonable hour. Parents shouldn't do that to their kids."

Blake turned to face her. He'd avoided looking at her for fear of seeing pity in her eyes. There were a lot of things he could take from her, but sympathy wasn't one. What he saw instead was anger. Strangely that helped. Made Blake feel like they were on the same page. "I'm not making excuses for what I did, Chloe. I'm not playing the poor pitiful me card. My dad was a lousy excuse for a person, but the choices I made were mine. Right or wrong, I can't blame him for what I did. All I can do is hope to make you understand why I stole the money, why I left."

She reached out and took his hand in hers, giving it an encouraging squeeze. "So tell me about that night."

"We'd told your mother we were going to the movies, but we actually snuck into that old shed behind your girlfriend's house."

Chloe laughed. "Her family was on vacation. You brought those sleeping bags and threw them on the floor. You'd bought a rose and scattered the petals on them. I thought it was all completely romantic."

He was glad she remembered that part of the night with fondness. "We were pretty damn horny most of the time."

"God," she joked. "That's a mild word for it. We were ravenous, insatiable. We couldn't walk three steps without touching and we couldn't touch without it sparking something hotter."

"I remember. We did it in two public restrooms, the backseat of your brother's car, no less than half a dozen times around this lake and God only knows where else."

"We were young. For me, sex was new. Sometimes, when I looked at you, it was almost painful how much I wanted you."

He understood that. He'd felt the same way back then. Hell, he'd felt that way since bumping into her two weeks ago. He went to bed every night with a physical ache caused by longing.

"You had to be home by midnight, but we were a little late."

Chloe nodded. "We were a lot late. I used the hidden key under the mat in the backyard, thinking I could sneak in through the back door in the kitchen.

"But Mama Lewis was sitting there, waiting for you. I was surprised that she didn't yell at us. Whenever I pissed my dad off, the whole neighborhood knew. He'd cuss me up one side and down the other, then finish it off with a punch or two."

Chloe winced. "My mother never hit me or my brothers. And she said yelling was never a good way to express an opinion."

"Yeah. She just looked at us and said she was disappointed. She explained how worried she'd been that we'd been in an accident. How much it would kill her to lose you. I swear I felt way worse after that conversation than I ever did when my dad yelled at me."

"Punishment through guilt and disappointment," Chloe said. "I totally intend to use it with my kids. It's very effective."

They laughed together quietly. Then Chloe sobered up. "You came back that night. You knew where we hid the key."

Blake nodded. "When I got back to my apartment, the neighbor was waiting for me. Said my dad had been arrested for getting into a fight. I figured he'd gotten drunk and punched some guy at a bar. It had happened before and the cops just made him sleep it off in the drunk tank, then sent him home the next day. The neighbor said this time was different. He said my dad was in real trouble and he needed money for bail. I dug through all my hiding spots, but I could only come up with about fifty bucks. I didn't have anyone else to ask."

"You didn't ask." There was no tone of accusation, just the statement of fact. He hadn't asked. He'd simply taken.

Blake blew out a long breath, then decided fuck it. He'd gone this far. It was time to say it all. "You're right. I didn't. I got back to your place. All the lights were out. Everybody was asleep. I used the key and I swear to you, I was going to sneak up to your room to see if you could loan me money, but…"

"But?" she prompted.

"I'd have to tell you why I needed it and I didn't want you to know my dad was a drunk loser in jail."

"Why not?"

"I was embarrassed. You were the best thing that had ever happened to me and the entire time we dated, I knew I didn't deserve you."

Chloe scowled. "That's bullshit."

He gave her a crooked grin. "I was a stupid nineteen-year-old kid. I'm not saying I was the sharpest tool in the shed. All I had going for me was my Harley, a lousy dead-end job in a sub shop and my pride. None of those things seemed like enough to keep a girl like you interested. I was in love with you, Chloe, and terrified of fucking everything up. Which I did anyway."

"So you walked into the house..." she began.

"Your mother's purse was on the kitchen table. Stealing wasn't exactly a new thing for me. I rifled through her wallet and found a couple hundred bucks. I was about to leave when I remembered the silver platter in the hutch in the dining room and I grabbed it too. And then I ran. You know, I've been wondering. How did you all know it was me who took the money?"

"You'd tucked some of those rose petals in your pocket before we left the shed. A few of them must have fallen out. I wouldn't have thought anything about it because you'd been in the kitchen when Mama found us sneaking in. But there were a couple by the hutch as well."

"Guess it's a good thing I became a cop. I clearly suck at covering my tracks as a thief."

Chloe smiled at his joke. "What happened after you left?"

"All hell broke loose."

"What do you mean?"

"I waited for the pawn shop to open the next morning. Took in your mom's platter and got a few hundred bucks for it. Then I went to the police station and bailed my dad out. I was stressing out over how I was going to find the money to buy the platter back. It was worth more than I realized. Anyway, my dad was in deep shit with some shady guys. He'd agreed to deliver some package, but he didn't."

"What was in the package?"

"Drugs. Never figured out if he sold them himself or had one hell of a party, but the package was gone and the guys wanted it or the money it would have brought in sales. They confronted my dad in the parking lot of a bar. Gave him a pretty good beat down. They took off when the cops showed up, but not before they told Dad he had twenty-four hours to produce the drugs or the money."

"Why was he arrested?"

Blake snorted, the sound betraying a bitterness he didn't like to show. "Even bloodied, my dad was a mean drunk. He took a swing at one of the cops. When they ran his name through the system, they found out he had some outstanding warrants. The second I sprung him from jail, he started making plans."

"What kind of plans?"

A rumble of thunder distracted them. Blake looked up at the sky. Afternoon was quickly turning to dusk and dark clouds were forming. Apparently the weathermen had been right. A storm was coming. They'd need to head back to the bike soon or risk getting wet. As it was, Blake wasn't sure they'd make it to the city before the rain started falling.

"Can we finish this at your place?"

Chloe looked up as well. He got the sense she wanted to finish what they'd started, but even she could see that wasn't going to happen here. "Sure."

Her tone gave him no hint to her feelings. Blake stood then offered her a hand. He didn't release it as they started walking back to his Harley. She didn't try to pull away. It gave him hope.

The ride back to Chloe's place felt less peaceful than the trip to the lake. For one thing, Blake couldn't put the bad memories away. Dredging up the past bothered him more than he'd expected. For years, he'd felt on top of his game, certain he'd kicked all the crap from his childhood to the curb. Clearly, he hadn't.

Secondly, the rain hadn't held off. They'd just made it

to the city limits when the sky opened up. By the time they reached Chloe's apartment, they were drenched from head to toe. He halfway expected her to tell him to take a hike. The afternoon by the lake had taken its toll and now they were cold and wet.

Instead, she pulled off her helmet, laughing as she lifted her face to the rain. "That was incredible. I couldn't decide if I was having fun or scared out of my wits. How could you see the road? That was a deluge."

He looked at her, raindrops sliding down her rosy cheeks, and felt like a two-ton truck had hit him. He grasped her face in his hands and, heedless of the storm that continued to pound down on them, he kissed her.

Chloe didn't resist. She simply wrapped her arms around his neck and kissed him back. Their tongues tangled as he ran his fingers through her hair. She pressed her chest closer to his, sharing her body warmth. He had no idea how long they stood on the city sidewalk, letting the rain pummel them as they kissed, but Blake could have stayed there forever.

Finally, common sense reared and he took a step back. "I know I said that motorcycle bag is waterproof, but we probably shouldn't tempt fate. You've got some expensive equipment in there."

She nodded as he unhooked the bag and threw the strap over his shoulder. She carried their helmets, leading the way upstairs to her apartment.

"You can put that bag over there." She pointed to the

corner of her studio. "I'll go grab some towels from the bathroom."

Blake set the bag down then hovered by the door. He was dripping all over her hardwood floors.

Chloe was back within seconds with an armload of fluffy towels. "Why are you standing there?"

He gestured at the puddle forming around his feet. "Didn't want to ruin your floor."

Chloe shrugged. "It's just water. It'll dry. Here." She held out a towel.

He crossed the room and took it from her. He ran it over his hair and face, then started undoing the buttons of his shirt. Chloe watched, making no move to stop him. Once he'd shrugged the clinging cotton off, she was there, rubbing all the water away with a towel.

When she finished, Blake reached for the hem of her t-shirt and tugged it over her head. Then he dried her as well. She sucked in a soft breath when he reached around her, unhooking her bra and adding it to the pile of wet clothing at their feet. He took his time, drying her breasts, loving the way her cold nipples budded even more at his touch.

Chloe reached for the button on his jeans and slowly slid the zipper down. He toed off his boots, chuckling as Chloe cursed in her struggles to strip the wet denim away. She followed the stubborn material down, kneeling before him as she gestured for him to lift one foot, then the other.

She peeled off his socks as well.

She made no attempt to rise. "Still go commando, I see."

He cupped her face in his palm, forcing her to look at him. "You're beautiful."

She gave him a wicked grin. "You're just trying to sweet talk me into giving you a blowjob."

He laughed. "Well, since you're down there anyway, it seems like a shame to—" His jest was cut short when Chloe grasped his cock, taking the head into her mouth without hesitation.

His hands flew to her hair. "Jesus, Chloe. I was kidding."

She didn't release him, just sucked him harder, deeper. Blake struggled to catch up. He'd been emotionally done in when they'd left the lake, then stressed out as he'd tried to get them home safely on the motorcycle during the storm. Now he was standing in Chloe's apartment, her lips wrapped around his cock, and his brain was scrambled, fried.

She cupped his balls in one palm, her other wrapped around the base. He recalled the first time she'd given him a blowjob. She'd dragged him into the back storeroom of the sub shop one night after closing and shocked him by asking him to teach her how to suck his dick.

Given the way she was driving him to the peak right now, he'd say she'd learned her lesson well. Increasing her speed, she took him deeper and deeper into her mouth with each pass. The head of his cock brushed the back of her throat. He tightened his grip on her hair, trembling slightly when she groaned, the vibrations adding another dimension to the blowjob.

"Chloe."

She looked up at him, her expression the perfect blend of mischief and dare. She'd turned the tables on him, grasping control, and now she was challenging him to take it back. If he hadn't been so mentally exhausted he would have called her to task immediately, pulling her over his knees.

Somehow she'd known. Known what he needed to make it through the next part. And she'd given it freely.

He tugged her hair more roughly than before. Chloe moaned again, her eyes closing in bliss. Her desire fueled his, gave him back the strength that had been waning. It wasn't time for this. Not yet. There was still more to say.

He pushed her mouth away. Chloe frowned and started to protest, but he put a firm finger beneath her chin, forcing her face up. "No. Not this way."

Blake lifted her slowly then placed his lips on hers. For several moments, they simply kissed. Then he moved, resting his forehead against hers. She shivered and he realized she was still wearing her wet jeans.

"Take off your pants. We need to get you dry and warm."

Chloe moved away only a few steps, slipping her own jeans off as Blake watched. She didn't have a shy bone in her body—never had—so her disrobing became part seduction. She turned her back to him before sliding the denim over her hips. She tugged her panties down at the same time, so when she bent forward to draw the material over her feet, he was treated to a bird's-eye view of her perfect ass.

Before he could think better of it, he reached over and slapped it. Chloe gasped—the sound more surprise than pain—then she grasped her ankles. "Do that again."

He considered making her beg. They had only started to explore their sexual kinks when he'd stolen that money and left town. Even so, he had recognized Chloe's desire for pain, her love of rough play and her need to be dominated. He'd spent too many lonely nights, jacking off in bed as he imagined all the ways he would have taken her if life hadn't thrown them the curveball.

Now, all those fantasies came rushing to the surface. He would make them a reality. But first…

He grasped her gently by the elbow and helped her up. She turned, confusion briefly flashing across her face before she understood.

"I'm sorry, Blake. I…"

He tugged her into his arms, holding her tightly. "I get the same way around you. I lose all sense of control. I just need to try to make things right between us before we let this go any further."

She nodded. "I agree."

He led her to the couch and they sat down together side by side. Chloe tugged an afghan from the ottoman and spread it out over top of them. It was cozy and warm.

"You said your dad was making plans after you bailed him out. To do what?"

"He was in big trouble with the drug pushers. We went back to our place and he started packing up our stuff. Within half an hour, we were back on the street. I'd worked at that crummy sub shop for nearly three years after school, saving enough money to buy my motorcycle. My dad went out that afternoon and stole one. By noon, we were on the highway, speeding away from New Orleans."

"Just like that?"

Blake rubbed the back of his neck. He'd spent countless hours trying to figure out why the hell he'd followed his father so easily, why he hadn't fought to stay. "I'd stolen from your mother, Chloe. I couldn't figure out a way to make that right."

"You could've explained it to me, Blake."

He lifted one shoulder. "I know. But my dad…"

"He couldn't stay in New Orleans. And you couldn't leave him."

"That was the biggest mistake I made that day. I chose to stay with the wrong person."

Chloe fell silent. Blake wasn't sure what else to say. At this point, the ball was in her court. Either she would forgive him. Or she wouldn't.

"You've been back in New Orleans for almost six years?"

He nodded.

"Did you come back to town with your dad?"

"No. My dad and I split ways about two years after we left." Blake didn't tell her about the near-rape or the fight. That was a story he'd take to his grave. "I'd been on the force nearly three years before I realized he'd come back to New Orleans too. Got a call when I was on duty. Drunk and disorderly. I walked into the bar in my uniform and sure enough, there he sat."

"That must have been an uncomfortable reunion."

Blake snorted. "You can't even imagine."

"Did you arrest him?"

Blake shook his head. "No. I drove him back to his place. Crazy asshole was actually proud of me for joining the force."

"Really?" Chloe asked. "I thought he hated cops."

"He's a twisted bastard. He believed he could use my position to cover up his crimes."

Chloe winced. "Wow."

"I pretended he could."

Her eyebrows rose. "What? Why?"

Blake had never admitted his reasons before. He wondered if Chloe would change her mind about him if she learned exactly how manipulative he was. "Entrapment. I set up a mini-sting with my captain. Pretended to be in cahoots with my father while gaining information about a local drug ring. I knew my dad hadn't changed his ways and I figured he'd be useful. He was."

"That couldn't have been easy for you."

Blake leaned his head against the back of the couch. "You'd be surprised."

She scowled. "Don't. Stop playing the tough guy. You put your dad in jail. And even if he was an asshole, he was the only parent you'd ever had."

Blake wrapped an arm around her shoulders, pulling her head to his chest. "The world is simpler when you look at it in black and white. If you start adding color into the equation…"

"Is that why you've never called me?"

Blake wasn't sure how to respond, so he stalled. "What?"

"You've been back in New Orleans for years. You saw my book. You knew I was still here. Why didn't you call me?"

She sounded so genuinely hurt, it made Blake's chest ache. "I didn't think you'd forgive me."

She lifted her head. "You were wrong."

He gave her a tentative grin, hope blossoming. "So you do forgive me?"

She shook her head.

His brow creased. "You don't?" For a moment, he felt lost. If she couldn't understand his reasons for stealing the money, everything they once had was truly lost.

"It doesn't matter if I forgive you, Blake. I'm pretty sure I stopped being mad at you the second my mother said you paid her the money back. I wouldn't have had sex with you otherwise."

He felt the urge to laugh, but his gut told him something was still wrong.

Chloe cupped his cheek in her hand. "It's not *my* forgiveness that matters. You have to forgive yourself, Blake. You stayed away because you were trying to do penance, right?"

Her words hit him like a ton of bricks. Had he done that? Had he let guilt for his actions stop him from searching for her, for happiness? For love? "I'm not sure what to say."

Chloe gave him a wicked grin that told him exactly how much of a fool he'd been to stay away. "You could always start with 'You're right'."

He chuckled. "I'm pretty sure I'd be smart to use those words sparingly."

She gave him a light punch on the arm. "Blake."

"You're right, Chloe. I've been letting guilt guide my decisions. I was wrong to do that."

Chloe leaned closer and kissed him, showing him with actions rather than words that all truly was forgiven between them. It was a gift Blake had never let himself hope for.

For the first time in six years, he felt like he'd truly come home.

Blake reached for her, pulling her onto his lap. He had obviously reached the same realization she had. The time for talking was over. One main benefit of the rain was it had helped them shed the clothes early on. Blake was naked, his skin warm against hers.

He kissed her gently at first. An apology. Chloe accepted it, offering her own in return. She was sorry for doubting him. For failing to believe in the man she'd known he was. Both of them had let pride and the exaggerated emotions of youth—the ones that believe every problem is insurmountable and the worst thing that could ever happen—take control.

Chloe met Blake's tongue halfway, letting the passion of the kiss build as she turned. Straddling his body, her knees on the cushions by his ass, she relished the hardness of his cock as it brushed her pussy, her stomach.

She'd spent too many years settling for lackluster sex. Chloe could see now she was to blame for those passionless affairs. Sex was way hotter when you were in love.

Love.

She broke the connection of their lips. She was wrong. There was still one more thing left to say.

Blake scowled at her retreat, clearly not finished. He started to pull her face back to his, but she resisted. "Chloe?"

"I love you."

His smile grew so wide, Chloe couldn't help but return it. "Say it again."

She lifted one eyebrow. "I think I'd be smart to use those words sparingly at first."

Blake laughed, shifting her until the head of his cock rested at the opening of her body. "I'll make it worth your while."

She glanced down, intent on taking her prize, with or without his permission. She started to slide down, but Blake's grip on her waist tightened, holding her in place. Dammit. She kept forgetting how strong he was.

When her gaze met his again, she saw something almost like sorrow in his eyes. "Blake?"

"I'm going to be greedy for a while, Chloe. I can't help it. I want too much from you."

She understood the sentiment. She shared it. "We'll be gluttons together. I love you. I love you so much it hurts. And if you ever try to leave me again, I will hunt you down to the end of the earth and I'll—"

Blake cut off her threat with a kiss. "Never gonna happen, but you know…there are laws against threatening a police officer."

She returned his kiss with interest, nipping his lower lip. "Oh yeah? Handcuff-worthy laws?"

Blake chuckled. "Definitely."

He loosened his grip on her waist, using his hands to guide her, drawing her body down onto his cock. Both of them gasped once he was fully seated. Her position on top left her wide open and able to take him deeper. It still didn't feel like enough.

She lifted up a few inches then slid back down slowly, savoring Blake's pained expression, his quick intake of air.

He gave her a warning look. "Are you really sure you want to play the control game, Chloe?"

She recognized the threat. She'd been trying to force his hand ever since they'd walked into the apartment, daring him to take charge.

Regardless of the danger, it was a challenge she couldn't refuse. After so many years apart, she felt the need to test him, to see if he was still the dominant lover she remembered. Craved.

However, she needed him to understand that she had changed. While she still wanted to submit to him, she wasn't the weak, inexperienced little girl he'd taken all those years ago. She wouldn't bend to his will easily. She intended to make him work for it.

Chloe rose once more, returning even slower, taking the time to tighten her inner muscles. Blake felt it. The stiffness of his posture told her that while he may appreciate her efforts, he was determined to come out on top.

She repeated her seductive slide a third time, adding her breasts to the game as she leaned forward, rubbing them against his face.

Blake's tenuous grip on control slipped a bit as his hands found her ass, his fingers digging into the flesh there. She expected him to try to seize power. After all, it was clear he needed her to move faster, harder. She wanted that too.

Unfortunately, the damn man was too astute. She should have known better than to play with a cop and his instincts. His grip on her ass loosened, though he didn't move them away. Instead, he reached farther around her, his fingers slipping into the crease.

She gasped when he parted the twin globes, dragging one finger lower.

Their sexual experiences ten years earlier had been cut short. Chloe had always wished there had been more time for them to explore their kinkier desires. Now, at last, there was.

"Who's in charge, Chloe?" His voice was deep, dark, tinged with a hint of menace.

She wasn't afraid. She smiled and continued her painfully slow glide up and down his cock. "I'm not sure."

He leaned closer, his teeth capturing one of her nipples. She gasped when he started to press down. She felt Blake's gaze on her face. One of the reasons she felt safe exploring these games with him was because she knew he would never let it go too far. He read her face, protected her…even from herself. Her hands tightened on his shoulders and he released her.

"Do you want to reconsider your answer?"

She bit her lip, pretending to think. Then she shook her head.

"Good girl."

She didn't understand his pleasure until he lifted her off his cock, twisted her quickly, and tossed her facedown over his lap. Before she could even consider escaping, his hand struck her bare ass three times. Chloe gripped Blake's calf, torn between halting the spanking and begging for more. It hurt more than she'd expected, but not so much that she couldn't feel her arousal sparking, flaring.

Blake stroked the heated flesh, his fingers surprisingly

gentle after his hard blows. Then he repeated the motions, striking her ass three more times before caressing the skin again.

Her stomach clenched in anticipation when he raised his hand, her body readying itself for more. He paused. She knew the game. He wanted her to ask for it, to beg. She lifted her head, glancing at him over her shoulder.

"Who's in charge, Chloe?"

She narrowed her eyes, not ready to give in yet. She let her silence answer the question.

Blake grinned at her stubbornness, clearly enjoying the struggle for power. He lifted her from his lap—much to her dismay—pulling her up until she straddled his lap once more.

He guided his cock to her pussy, using a strong grip on her waist to press himself inside her. Fully seated, he held her in place, refusing to let her move.

"Are you on the Pill?"

She nodded.

"Are you okay with not using the condom?"

"Yes."

His strong hands held her down despite her attempts to move. She needed friction, thrusting, anything. Her pussy clenched against his cock, seeking more, but Blake held steady.

"Blake," she snapped, her temper firing. "Fuck me. Now."

He leaned toward her, nipping her earlobe in warning. "That's not a very nice way to ask. Who's in charge, Chloe?"

She continued her struggle, wiggling her hips as much as his hands would allow…which wasn't anywhere near enough.

"Hand the reins over to me and I'll give you everything you want."

It was the most tempting offer she'd ever received in her life. Given her rather powerful personality, she'd only managed to attract men who expected her to control every aspect of her life—professionally, personally…and sexually. She was damn tired of being on top.

Still, her pride made it hard for her to give in so easily. Even if she was cutting off her nose to spite her face. It was on the tip of her tongue to tell him what he wanted to hear, but Blake must have decided her time was up.

He lifted her off his cock then grasped her hand in his. He tugged her to her bed, where he pulled back the covers and tossed her into the middle of the mattress. She started to sit, but he held his hand up, halting her.

"Don't move. Not one muscle. If you do, I'm going to demonstrate the difference between a spanking to stimulate and a spanking to punish. Understand?"

She nodded, the sadist in her really wanting to test that limit. Instead, she decided to let this game play out. She lay on the bed and watched as he rifled through her dresser. He found what he was seeking in the second drawer.

Chloe closed her eyes, fighting her growing arousal when he came back to the bed, scarves in hand. He used one to bind her wrists together then he tied them outstretched above her to the headboard. She wiggled, trying to loosen the knot, but Blake knew his stuff.

She startled, her gaze flying to his face when his hands pressed her legs apart and he knelt between them. She read his intent as he looked down at her pussy. He looked a bit like a man surveying the all-you-can-eat bar. She giggled.

Blake paused, his mouth quirking up at the corners. "You find bondage funny?"

She shook her head. "Not really. I'm excited and edgy. My mind is whirling a million miles a minute, thinking about ridiculous things. I'm a nervous giggler."

"Maybe I should try to distract you." With that, he bent down, his tongue finding her clit on the first stroke.

Her hips reared up, but Blake's hands were there, holding her against the mattress. Though he hadn't restrained her feet, Chloe didn't pretend that she wasn't truly helpless. Blake had complete control of her body, his own personal plaything. That idea didn't frighten her at all. It made her even hotter.

Blake ran his tongue along her slit from ass to clit and back again. She felt consumed, possessed. Chloe closed her eyes, but that didn't stop her from feeling Blake's head shake.

"No, Chloe. Open your eyes. Watch me."

She obeyed. The command forced her to see as well as feel. It was a potent combination. Most men viewed this act as a chore. Blake clearly did not. He pressed his tongue inside her pussy and she bit her lip, fighting not to come so quickly. She was trying to play hard to get, but that game would only work if she didn't have an orgasm every time Blake looked in her direction.

Then she wondered why she was resisting. Blake was a very generous lover, never stopping when she'd come just once. She released a long breath and gave herself over to the magic of his lips, tongue and fingers. She was seconds away from complete bliss when Blake pulled away.

She frowned. "Wait."

"Who's in charge, Chloe?"

Damn him. He had her over a barrel and he knew it. She didn't bother to protest. This game was over before it started. "You are."

He smiled, the expression transforming his entire face. He was so handsome he took her breath away. The tight lines around his mouth, the haunted look in his eyes had faded. She suspected it would take some time before they vanished for good. Maybe they never would. Given

Blake's painful childhood, perhaps he'd never totally escape the bad memories. But she sure as hell intended to distract him for the next fifty years or so.

"Remember you said that." He spoke lightly enough, but there was something behind the warning that triggered alarm bells.

"Okay."

"You're not to come without permission."

And that was the sound of the other shoe falling. He gave her a wicked wink then resumed his place between her legs, driving her arousal higher and higher, while offering no reprieve.

She was trembling and panting, begging, but Blake ignored her. His tongue wiggled against her clit as he drove three fingers inside her, deep and hard. Just when she knew she'd fail, he withdrew, giving her time to recover before starting the same glorious torture over. And over. When he dragged one wet finger lower, pressing it just inside her anus, she felt a tear slide down her cheek.

"Blake. Please."

Chloe wasn't sure what he heard in her voice, but he lifted his head. "Come, baby."

With that, he pushed the finger at her ass in all the way while pressing his tongue inside her pussy. She thrashed and cried out loudly as her body exploded into a million bright, shiny pieces.

The moment she came down, Blake was there. He untied her arms then thrust his cock in with one strong push. She was back up in an instant, her body reacting to his hard fucking as if she hadn't just had the most incredible orgasm in the history of sex.

She wrapped her arms around his neck and her legs about his waist. She wasn't sure why she felt the need to cling to him. Maybe she was still harboring some fears of her own. She didn't believe he'd leave her again, but even as she thought it, she realized her heart wouldn't survive losing him.

"Love you," she whispered, the words coming out in a harsh pant as Blake drove into her like a man possessed.

How long would it take the two of them to feel confident that this time it would stick, it would last?

"I love you, Chloe. God, so much. So fucking much." As he spoke, he stroked her clit, her hot button. He played her body like a violin. Her back arched as she screamed. Best of all, Blake was right there with her. He stiffened, jet after jet of come filling her.

Once they recovered, Blake fell to her side, his arm wrapped loosely around her waist. "Damn. I always thought I'd built our sexcapades up in my mind over the years. Made them bigger than they really were."

Chloe laughed, turning to face him. "I thought the same thing."

"It's actually better than I remembered. Off the

charts. I swear I thought my cock was going to explode."

She moved her face closer, the two of them rubbing noses playfully. "We're quite a pair."

"Yeah. We sure are. I should warn you. I still have my fair share of pride. I'm just a bit better about keeping it contained."

She grinned, kissing him lightly. "Well, my temper is just as bad as ever and I'm not even trying to keep it under control. You're just gonna have to deal."

Blake ruffled her hair. "Yeah, I've noticed that. I'm not worried. I have a feeling we're going to be okay from this point on."

"I wouldn't say that."

"What do you mean?"

She lifted one shoulder. "We're going to have to break the news that we're dating again to my brothers."

Blake fell to his back and released a long breath. "Damn. We were so close to that happy ending."

She giggled, punching his shoulder. "Chicken shit. You can break it to them at Sunday dinner."

Blake rolled toward her, pulling her underneath him as he slid into her once more. "Okay. But I'm warning you right now. I'm bringing my gun."

FROM BIG EASY NIGHTS AVAILABLE NOW

"Open your legs. I want to see exactly how wet you are." Justin tugged on her knee as he issued the command, then felt Ned's hand on the other. Her thighs parted easily as her skirt inched higher. She tried to tug it down, but Ned caught her wrist, his voice deep, stern.

"Leave it."

"Ned," she whispered, uncertainty creeping in again. There was a difference between talking and doing. They'd test her limits tonight, push her completely out of her comfort zone.

Justin leaned closer, trying to set her mind at ease. Ned was always too intense, his need to control a woman coming out stronger, darker. While Justin didn't think Bella was balking, she was still a novice and probably not completely confident in her decision to pursue this adventure. "Trust us, Bells. We'll never hurt you."

Her expression cleared, showing him just how much faith she had in them. It twisted Justin's insides, made him warm, happy.

She touched his face gently. "I do trust you. Completely. I wouldn't be here otherwise."

Unable to resist any longer, Justin ran his hand along the inside of her leg. He sat close enough to hear her sharp intake of breath. The heat of her pussy hit him before his fingers reached their goal. Their girl was on fire.

Then he hit pay dirt. Bella's eyes closed as he stroked his finger along her slit. She was heat and moisture and sex incarnate.

Ned leaned closer. "Don't close your eyes, Bella. Look at what's happening on that stage."

Bella lifted her eyelids slowly and he watched her struggle to focus. Justin studied her face and realized when she recognized what was happening in the performance.

"She misbehaved," Ned whispered as Justin circled her clit. Bella bit her lip so tightly, he worried she'd split the skin and draw blood.

Ned continued to talk about the show onstage. "Her teacher is angry with her. He's punishing her."

The actor onstage—the professor—had bent his naughty schoolgirl over his desk and taken out a ruler. The scene was an old, familiar one, but Justin could tell from

Bella's responses it was speaking to some hidden desires. Did she like the idea of being punished by an authority figure?

She slid down on her chair—just a little, but enough—to allow Justin better access to her pussy. He didn't accept her invitation, determined to crank the heat even higher. While the silent actions of her body told him she wanted a stronger touch, he wouldn't give in until she was pleading, begging. He dragged his finger over her clit once more, making the touch lighter this time.

She groaned softly.

"We'll punish you the same way the next time you're late to work."

Bella's gaze jerked to Ned's face. No doubt she wanted to reiterate the time limit she'd placed on this encounter, but neither of them was in the mood to continue that pretense. Justin pressed on her clit again, distracting her before moving lower to circle the entrance to her pussy.

Bella's breathing became more labored. Between Justin's touches and Ned's dirty promises, she appeared to be losing her grip, relinquishing control of her inhibitions.

"We'll pull you into my office, bend you over the desk, lift your skirt and yank down your panties."

"I don't wear skirts to work," Bella whispered, though it was clear she was turned-on by Ned's story.

"You will from now on. We're changing the dress

code for you."

She looked as if she would argue, so Justin went for more distraction, pressing the tip of his finger into her wet pussy.

She closed her eyes, her expression betraying how much she loved this. She gave herself up to the moment.

"I'll pull a ruler out of my desk drawer and Justin and I will take turns spanking you. I want to see that sexy ass of yours blush as prettily as your cheeks are right now."

Justin pressed his finger deeper, realizing Ned's fantasy wasn't just working against Bella. His cock was so stiff it hurt. The tight clench of her pussy didn't help. She felt like heaven.

Ned added more fuel to the fire building in her body. "Once we've finished punishing you, we'll take turns fucking you from behind. You're going to spend hours with our cocks inside you from now on, beauty."

ABOUT THE AUTHOR

Writing a book was number one on Mari Carr's bucket list and on her thirty-fourth birthday, she set out to see that goal achieved. Now her computer is jammed full of stories — novels, novellas, short stories and dead-ends. A New York Times and USA TODAY bestseller as well as winner of the Passionate Plume, Mari finds time for writing by squeezing it into the hours between 3 a.m. and daybreak when her family is asleep and the house is quiet.

You can visit Mari's website at www.maricarr.com.

ALSO BY MARI CARR

Trinity Masters

Elemental Pleasure

Primal Passion

Scorching Desire

Forbidden Legacy

Sparks in Texas

Sparks Fly

Big Easy

Blank Canvas

Crash Point

Full Position

Rough Draft

Big Easy Heat

Big Easy Nights

Second Chances

Fix You

Full Moon

Status Update

Big Easy Heat

The Back-Up Plan

Never Been Kissed

Wine & Moonlight

Compass Brothers

Northern Exposure

Southern Comfort

Eastern Ambitions

Western Ties

Love's Compass

Compass Girls

Winter's Thaw

Hope Springs

Summer Fling

Falling Softly

Black & White Collection

Erotic Research

Tequila Truth

Rough Cut

Happy Hour

Power Play

Slam Dunk

Mari Carr

Naughty is Nice

In the Running

Learning Curves

Dangerous Curves

Wicked Curves

Just Because

Because of You

Because You Love Me

Because It's True

Just Because

Cowboys

Spitfire

Rekindled

Inflamed

Lowell High

Retreat

Covert Lessons

Mad about Meg

Wild Irish

Come Monday

Ruby Tuesday

Waiting for Wednesday

Sweet Thursday

Friday I'm in Love

Saturday Night Special

Any Given Sunday

Wild Irish Christmas

June Girls

No Recourse

No Regrets

Made in the USA
Charleston, SC
18 May 2016